To all the kids whose hands
sweat and hearts pound when
they get up in front of the class

AMANDA PANITCH

IT'S MY PARTY AND I DON'T WANT TO GO

■SCHOLASTIC

Published in the UK by Scholastic Children's Books, 2020
Euston House, 24 Eversholt Street, London, NW1 1DB
A division of Scholastic Limited

London – New York – Toronto – Sydney – Auckland
Mexico City – New Delhi – Hong Kong

First published in the US by Scholastic Inc., 2020
Text © Amanda Panitch, 2020

The right of Amanda Panitch to be identified as the author of this work has
been asserted by her under the Copyright, Designs and Patents Act 1988.

ISBN 978 0702 30492 7

A CIP catalogue record for this book is available from the British Library.

Printed by CPI Group (UK) Ltd, Croydon, CR0 4YY
Papers used by Scholastic Children's Books are made from wood
grown in sustainable forests and other controlled sources.

1 3 5 7 9 10 8 6 4 2

www.scholastic.co.uk

CHAPTER 1

It all started because I was afraid of a cake. It would be a lot less embarrassing if I said the cake was poisoned or really a meat loaf covered in mashed potatoes pretending to be a cake (gross), but no. It was just a plain, boring chocolate cake.

"I'll go up with you if you want," Zoe whispered. We sat straight in our chairs, trying not to wrinkle our fancy dresses. They both had big poufy skirts that crinkled when we moved and sleeves that hung loosely to our elbows, only mine was purple and hers was green.

The whole room applauded. Not for Zoe—they were all staring at the front of the room, where my big sister, Hannah, stood behind that terrifying cake. Some of her friends smiled by her side, their braces glinting in the light from all the candles and the flashes from the professional camera.

Beads of sweat popped all across my forehead. Because soon she'd call *me* up to smile by her side and light one of those candles. Up in front of the room. In front of all two hundred and forty-seven eyes (and Uncle Barry's eye patch, which was somehow even more intimidating than an extra staring eyeball). All judging every move I made. Against Hannah. And against my pretty, popular older sister, what would they think of me?

". . . to light candle number ten, my younger sister, Eliana!" Hannah announced with a gleaming smile.

I raised my hands to clap, but they stopped midair. Eliana? Already?

That was me.

"My younger sister, Eliana!" Hannah repeated through clenched teeth. Those two hundred and forty-seven eyes and one eye patch spun around the room, searching for me. I froze in place, breath catching in my throat.

"MY YOUNGER SISTER, ELIANA!" Hannah was getting a little screechy now, the way she got when I was dawdling and making her late for theater club or debate team. You didn't want to get in Hannah's way when she got like that. That was how you got her lines screamed in your ear while you were just trying to get ready.

"Ellie! Go!" Zoe gave me a little push. By the time I stumbled to my feet, the whole room had found me. I felt every one of those eyes piercing me like a thumbtack, trying to pin me to a giant invisible bulletin board.

They already had to be wondering what was taking me so long, which was bad enough. I knew what else they were probably thinking. *Why's she moving so slow? What's wrong with her? Why does she look so stupid? Especially compared to that sister of hers?*

My whole body was running with sweat when I made it to Hannah, and the fire from all those candles just made it worse. "Finally, Ellie!" Hannah hissed. She was still smiling beneath the glossy pink lipstick she was allowed to wear for special occasions. "Are you okay?" She didn't wait for me to answer. "Unless you're dying, light your candle before the whole cake's covered in wax."

She handed me a candle. I touched it to the flame, and it blazed to life. I let out a long breath, making it shiver. Light a candle. I could do this.

Except the only empty candles were way on the other side of the cake. What genius had decided to light the closer candles first, meaning that any latecomers had to stretch their arms alllll the way over a field of fire? I'd never really thought about how I was going to die before, but now I knew. I could see my own obituary:

```
Eliana Rachel Katz, age almost-eleven,
went up in flames Saturday night in
front of an enormous crowd of people.
Her mother said tearfully, "I shouldn't
have made her get that itchy dress off
the clearance rack! If only I'd let
her get the soft, silky, and much less
flammable one off the mannequin, she'd
be alive today." Other guests said,
less tearfully, "Who?" Because nobody
could ever possibly stop celebrating
Hannah for any reason whatsoever,
guests did the conga line over the
deceased's charred body.
```

An elbow bit me in the side. I jumped. The candle wobbled in my hand, shaking loose a big glob of wax. It hit the table, just barely missing my hand. My heart thudded. I didn't have to look up to know that all those eyes were still staring at me, judging everything I did. I could feel them prickling.

"Ellie, stop spacing out!" It was truly amazing how Hannah could whisper and screech at the same time.

I couldn't ruin my only sibling's bat mitzvah. I could do this. I raised my candle, taking a deep breath to fill me up with courage . . .

. . . only it kind of felt like I'd inhaled the fire instead. It filled me up, scorching my lungs and my ribs and my stomach, making the chicken fingers and fries I'd eaten earlier bubble unpleasantly. It left no room for any air. Just my heart, pounding against my ribs as if it were trying to escape.

I sucked in another breath, but it only fanned the flames. For my next one, I took such a big breath that it wheezed in the back of my throat. I tried another, then another. It didn't help. Could I suffocate to death while I was still breathing?

I gulped air, then choked. Black speckles danced at the corners of my vision. My knees wobbled. My mind was blank, but somewhere a tiny, desperate voice pleaded, *Don't fall into the cake of fire.*

That cursed cake. *I knew there was a reason to be afraid of you.*

I barely felt Hannah prying the candle from my hand, even though she had to unstick each finger individually. They'd all gone totally numb. Once she'd taken the candle, she grabbed my hand in hers and raised them both above her head. "Stage fright," she called. The crowd laughed. Somehow, that fanned the flames inside me worse than any of my breaths had, making them jump wildly.

They were going to eat me alive.

I must have missed Hannah lighting the candle, because suddenly she was nudging me gently to the side and reading a new poem that would invite our parents up to light their own candle. Her words echoed in the emptiness between my ears, as if I were hearing them from the other end of a long tunnel. I tottered off to the side of the dance floor, and I definitely would have fallen over if Zoe hadn't suddenly appeared to catch me.

"Those heels. Hard to walk in them," she told a group of distant cousins who were staring at me like I'd sprouted a second head from my shoulder. Then she whispered, "It's okay, Ellie. Lean on me."

I did lean on her, all the way out of the big main room and into the hallway to the bathrooms. There, Zoe and I sagged together against the flowered wallpaper and sank to the dirty green carpet. I traced where the wallpaper met the floor. It was peeling along the bottom. I pulled a strip loose and let it curl to the floor.

"Ellie, what's wrong?" Zoe whispered frantically.

The world around me was getting fuzzy. I closed my eyes so that I wouldn't have to see Zoe watching me die. Blackness swamped me, which was surprisingly soothing. Maybe that was also due to the fact that we'd finally escaped all those staring eyes. Nobody was watching me except Zoe, who didn't really count as a person.

I mean that in the best possible way. I've known her forever. My family's condo was across the hall from her family's condo until we were eight, when both our families bought houses and moved out. So we grew up running back and forth between our unlocked doors, grabbing food out of each other's refrigerators, and sleeping in each other's beds. We used to tell people we were identical twins, which would get us funny looks considering Zoe's Black and I'm about as white as you can get.

Zoe said, "It's going to be okay," but there was still panic in her voice. "You have to breathe, or you're going to pass out."

I am, I wanted to tell her, but I couldn't get any words out over the whistling sounds of my gasping and gasping and gasping.

"I think you're hyperventilating," she said. "This happened to my dad after my grandma died. It's not good!"

I wished I were capable of screaming at her, *I know it's not good! I'm the one who can't breathe!*

"Are you having a panic attack or something?"

A panic attack? Seriously? If I could've shouted at her, I'd've done it then. Because this wasn't mere panic. This was something way more than panic. I'd panicked before, feeling nervous before a test and worrying that I'd fail. This wasn't panic—this was something physical.

The soothing blackness and the quiet were already starting to help, though. Some of the flames inside me died down, leaving a little room for air. I tried to tell Zoe so, but my throat was still too strangled to speak.

I had no idea how long we sat there. I thought I was going to die. But eventually the flames shrank until they were nothing but a pile of cool ashes sitting atop my diaphragm.

I opened my eyes, squinting at the light. "I'm alive."

"Thank goodness," Zoe said.

As if the partygoers could hear us, a roar of applause swelled in the big room. I pushed myself to my feet, cringing at how the sweat had gone all cold and sticky on my skin. "We should get back in there."

Zoe rose, too, her dark eyes full of concern. "Are you sure?"

I rolled my shoulders till they cracked. "Yeah. I'll be fine now." And I would be, I knew it. Because I wouldn't have to get back in front of the crowd or talk to anyone I didn't know. I could just hide in the back with Zoe and eat cake. And after all that cake had done to me, I *wanted* to slice it open and chew and swallow it.

"What about your own bat mitzvah?" Zoe murmured as we reentered the banquet hall.

I had no idea what to say back to that. Fortunately, it was just then that the DJ broke out the bright stomping beat of "Hava Nagila." We had no choice but to step onto the dance floor and get sucked into the hora, swirling round and round in circles with all the other guests.

Hannah was in the middle, getting hoisted into the air on a chair. Nobody was looking at me, which was fine. I was just one of many.

My mom danced by me, twisting down to look at me before she sailed past. "You okay?"

I forced a smile. No way I was going to let on that I couldn't even handle something small like lighting a candle. "Yeah! Totally fine! Just had to run to the bathroom."

She gave a little laugh like we were sharing a secret. "Eat too many sliders?"

I managed to force a whole laugh before she disappeared back into the crowd. *See? Look how fine I am. More than fine. I'm just peachy.*

Still, as Hannah got lifted up and down on the chair in the middle of the dance floor, Zoe's words crawled through my mind. *What about your own bat mitzvah?* It was a valid question. After all, I barely had to do anything for Hannah's bat mitzvah—just get up in front of the crowd and light a stupid candle with her. And I couldn't even handle that. That evil cake sent me into a spiral of fear. How was I going to spend the whole *day* in front of all those eyes, and not just lighting candles, either—singing in Hebrew, making speeches, and smiling for pictures?

Don't worry. That's almost two whole years away, I told myself firmly as the crowd rushed to bring our hands to the center of the dance floor, then swooped back out. *You have plenty of time to figure out a plan.*

Over the next year and a half, I tried to figure out ways I could possibly do everything that would be required of me as a bat mitzvah girl. The only conclusion I came to?

The only way I wouldn't freak out during my bat mitzvah was if there *was* no bat mitzvah.

CHAPTER 2

It's never a good thing when you overhear your parents saying your name in the other room, followed by a "Shhhh!" You know the only thing that means? They're talking about you, and they don't want you to know. Maybe they're saying, "Is it time to tell Ellie about our upcoming move to frozen Siberia?"

I shivered. I didn't like the cold. My dad didn't like winter, either. I didn't want to wear my puffy winter jacket all the time. It made me look like the Abominable Snowman! So why would we move to Siberia? It didn't make any sense.

Okay, maybe I was getting ahead of myself. I should find out what was *really* going on. I kept walking down the hallway and stuck my head inside the living room.

Mom and Dad were sitting on the couch, mugs of coffee on the table in front of them. As soon as they saw me, they raised those mugs to their mouths and took a sip. Probably to hide their guilty faces.

But when they lowered them, they just looked normal. Bored, even. "What's happening, Ells?" Dad asked.

I glanced around the room. Nothing seemed off. The posed family photos of the four of us we took every year still hung on the wall. Pictures from Hannah's bat mitzvah, almost two years ago now, dotted the wall above the couch. Embarrassing naked baby pictures of Hannah and me still decorated the mantel above the nonworking fireplace. Folders and papers were spread out on the coffee table, brown rings on them from the coffee mugs. "What are those?" I asked suspiciously.

Mom's glasses slipped down her nose as she looked at me. "We realized this morning that we only have four months until your bat mitzvah!"

Dad did a fake sniff. "Better enjoy the four months you have left of your childhood."

Mom rolled her eyes. "Anyway, we figured we should get planning seriously. We have the venue reserved, of course, but we have so much else to do."

My blood seemed to freeze in my veins. Which was perfect, because it meant I'd be right at home in Siberia. Living in an eternal winter seemed way more fun than thinking about my bat mitzvah, considering I hadn't come any closer to figuring out how I was going to put the brakes on this whole thing.

Then again, maybe I could use this impromptu family meeting to my advantage. If I knew what they were planning, I'd know exactly what I had to do to sabotage said plans. I couldn't just come out and tell my parents that I didn't want a bat mitzvah. They'd look at me all confused and disappointed, and wonder why I couldn't be more like Hannah. I'd had enough of people wondering why I couldn't be more like Hannah, thank you very much.

I smiled brightly. "Tell me everything."

Just as my dad opened his mouth, footsteps tapped through the door behind me. I held back a groan. Only one person had such perky footsteps. And okay, there was only one other person who lived in the house. But it was still the footsteps that told me Hannah had come in.

I had plenty of time to learn every single mannerism Hannah had. Watching her finish her rehearsals with the drama club. Watching her practice for debate team.

Watching her work on the talent show committee. She did everything that could possibly put her in front of a cheering crowd. And I was part of that cheering crowd.

Well, if one person sitting in the back row met the technical definition of a crowd. And I never actually cheered, either, because then I might cheer too loudly and people would turn around and then everybody would know I was there.

She'd told me more than once, "Ellie, you don't have to just sit here and watch me rehearse. You're in middle school now. Why don't you pick an activity, too?" She'd toss her hair, sending her shiny brown curls bouncing like she was in a shampoo commercial. "You should join the drama club! I can put in a good word for you with Mrs. Miller."

I'd just turn away and stare at the wall until Hannah got the hint and huffed away. Really, *I* was the one who should have been huffing. It was like Hannah looked at me through a pair of glasses made out of mirrors—she didn't see me, just herself reflected back.

And yeah, maybe Hannah and I looked like each other—we were both pale and short, with a bump in the middle of our noses and thick dark eyebrows—but under those looks, she might as well have been challah French toast while I was dry, crunchy matzah.

I almost signed my name up for the photography club—where I could be behind the camera, not in front of it—when the teacher passed around the sheet at the beginning of the school year, but I'd ended up leaving nothing but a pencil dot on the page. Because I couldn't risk it. There was always the chance the teacher would ask me to get up in front of the group and demonstrate something or talk about myself.

"Did I overhear that you're planning Ellie's bat mitzvah?" Hannah said, her voice way brighter than my smile could ever be. "I want in!"

She didn't wait for an invitation. Or even a reply. She just marched right in and plopped herself between Mom and Dad on the couch, bowing her head over the papers on the table. Which left me hovering awkwardly in the middle of the room, with not enough room on the couch for me to join them. I scowled at her, but she was too busy reading the papers to notice.

Which was just as usual, really. For my birthday last year, Hannah had made me a photo board for my wall. It was huge, bigger than the headboard of my bed, all covered with pictures of the two of us. Foam purple letters spelled out SISTERS on top.

She didn't notice, even after hours of sorting through pictures and printing them and arranging them, that in most of them, the only one smiling was her. So why would I expect her to notice that now?

"So we already booked the venue months ago," Mom said. She pushed her glasses up. "The same country club you had your bat mitzvah at, Hannah."

"Oh good, I liked that place," Hannah said.

"Right, and it fit everyone without costing a fortune." Mom flipped to the next folder in the spread. "We need to order invitations from the printer ASAP."

"Nobody can come if they don't get invited!" Dad said. He and Hannah laughed, but I didn't take it as a silly dad joke. It was true, right? If the invitations didn't go out and people didn't know about the bat mitzvah, nobody would show up.

I added a note to my mental list. Two notes, really. Invitations and venue. I had to be thorough. It could be easy for them to fix one thing that went wrong, less easy to fix a whole bunch of problems.

Mom said, "You liked your DJ, right, Hannah?"

"Sure."

"Okay." Mom scribbled something down on her note-pad. So did I. Well, I scribbled a mental note. "We'll give him a call and make sure he's free on the date. Hopefully he is."

"Ellie will be able to meet with him, right?" Hannah turned to me for the first time. I had been starting to think she assumed Mom and Dad had purchased an oddly lifelike Ellie statue as a gift for my bat mitzvah. "That was really helpful before my bat mitzvah. I got to tell him all my favorite songs and games and give him a list of what *not* to play."

She glanced sideways at my dad, who grinned. He had a whole song and dance routine to the old country song "Achy Breaky Heart," which would under no circum-stances be performed at my bat mitzvah. I mean, there would under no circumstances *be* a bat mitzvah, but priorities.

"Of course." Mom scribbled another note. So did I. "That leaves the caterers, right? At least for the big things we need to worry about for the moment. We'll need to order prizes for the games and make centerpieces, but those can be done closer to the date."

Hannah wrinkled her nose. "I didn't like my bat mitzvah food very much."

Neither had I. Who liked cold, soggy chicken fingers and limp French fries? Well, the French fries were still kind of good, but to be fair, French fries are always good, in any form, at any temperature. Go ahead, fight me on that. Except not really, because I have noodle arms and would definitely lose.

"Too bad," Mom replied. "Goldblum Catering is the only kosher caterer in the area, so we have to use them. They'd better not be booked already."

The only kosher caterer in the area. That meant that if for some reason they couldn't do my bat mitzvah, we'd have no other options for food. Meaning: bat mitzvah canceled.

"The rest is all on Ellie." All three of them turned and smiled at me at once. It was a little creepy. "Singing the haftorah and Torah portions and writing some great speeches!"

"I'll help you with the speeches," Hannah chimed in.

I gave her a small smile in return. That actually was a nice thing of her to offer. And speeches were her specialty. Being up in front of people in general was her specialty. (Mine? Being so quiet some kids in my class still didn't know my name by the end of the year.) Maybe I was too hard on her. She was trying to help, even if she wasn't quite getting it. I could've gotten stuck with a big sister who beat me up or rolled her eyes at me all the time, so really, I didn't have it so—

"It does sound like a good idea," Mom was musing. Wait. What sounded like a good idea? "I hated the idea of you two sitting around the house all day doing nothing the whole summer."

My face paled. This didn't sound good. Sitting around the house all day doing nothing was the best part of summer.

Hannah clapped her hands together. That also didn't sound good. Generally the things that made Hannah happy made me cringe. "It's going to be so fun, Ellie!"

"What?" I said, my voice heavy with dread.

She boggled at me. "Volunteering at the senior center with me and the USY kids! Were you not listening?"

Oh no, no, no. My breaths started coming quicker and quicker, kind of like Zoe's dog—Dogzilla—when he did any amount of running. This was a disaster. Volunteering with USY, the Jewish youth group that Hannah belonged to, at the senior center meant not just hanging out with Hannah and her equally as chatty friends (do you know how many times I've been asked, "Why are you so quiet?"), but having to *talk* to random old people. Like, a lot. As in, that was the entire point of Hannah volunteering there. To talk to them and keep them company.

Oh no, I thought, but it accidentally came out of my mouth, too.

A flash of hurt crossed Hannah's face. "I thought it would be fun. We don't get to spend much time together now that we're in different schools, and since we're both so busy . . ."

I wasn't busy. *Hannah* was busy. There was a big difference.

But Mom was squinting at me in the way that said, *I have set my mind on this thing and will achieve it, so help me God*, which meant I had only a second to head her off. I chose that over arguing with Hannah.

"I already have plans to volunteer with Zoe," I said quickly.

Mom's eyes unsquinted. "Doing what?"

Um. Um. Um. *Think, Ellie, think.*

I swear, there was not a single thought bouncing

around in my skull. Only the theme song of a cartoon I hadn't watched since I was five. Why? Good question, brain.

Wait. We'd gone to an assembly on one of the last days of school. One of the town librarians had come in and talked to us about summer volunteering programs at the library. I hadn't been listening, because Zoe and I had been texting each other about how Danny Cohen had accidentally brushed her arm in the hallway (or had it been on purpose??? Zoe wondered) but how could I go wrong with the library? The library was quiet. I could handle shelving books and choosing books to put on display and . . . whatever else librarians did. "Working at the library."

Hannah's face relaxed. "Oh, some of my friends did that in middle school."

Right. Okay. "Sorry I forgot to tell you," I said to Mom. "I have the flyer they gave us in my backpack somewhere." Along with a banana that was now probably rotten mush, I realized, but I could deal with that later. Also something I'd have to deal with later: telling Zoe that I'd volunteered her for volunteering. She might not exactly be thrilled. I liked the library, but she had big plans for the summer to train Dogzilla to win the Westminster Dog Show. I'd told her a lot that Dogzilla didn't really have the form or the youth to even enter, but it hadn't changed her mind.

"That sounds great, then," Mom said. "As long as you're not just sitting around the house."

"Right," said Dad. "Or standing, or dancing, or playing the piano."

"We don't have a piano," said Hannah.

"Even more reason why you shouldn't be playing one," Dad said. "I don't want either of you stealing a piano."

I shook my head. I had to call Zoe before my mom called her parents. Off to my room. Fortunately my parents didn't tell me to come back and keep talking about bat mitzvah stuff. Which was good. Because after I called Zoe, I had a plan to make. And not just any plan. This plan had to be foolproof. One hundred percent perfect. No way it could fail.

I had my own checklist. The same checklist as my parents', in fact. Only they were looking to build. And I was going to destroy.

Game. On.

CHAPTER 3

"That's a terrible idea," Zoe said. I'd just finished telling her about my foolproof, one-hundred-percent-perfect, no-way-it-can-fail plan. "In fact, it might just be the worst idea I've heard in my entire life. And my brother once thought that farting the national anthem would get him into the school talent show."

I remembered that. Mrs. Miller had almost thrown up. "What did you miss about the foolproof, one-hundred-percent-perfect, no-way-it-can-fail part?"

"What about how your last foolproof-whatever plan ended with us *here*?" She swept her arm around her, indicating the front of the town library. They'd built it when we were in fourth grade, so it was all shiny glass and new carpet. "Instead of at home in bed?"

She had a point. "Thanks for doing this, by the way," I said sincerely. She'd groaned on the phone when I told her about this whole volunteering thing, but I reminded her that she seriously owed me after getting me in trouble a few months ago, when she blamed me for leaving the freezer open after our super-secret midnight sundae plan. "Maybe it won't be so bad."

She sighed so hard it was like she was trying to get rid of all the air in her body. "Maybe. Okay, let's go in."

Inside, she asked the librarian behind the front desk where to go, and he pointed toward the back. We strolled through crowds of people using the public computers, tall shelves of books upon books, and the teen section with its beanbag chairs. "Anyway, about your plan," Zoe said. "It is definitely *not* foolproof or whatever. Do you seriously think your parents will just shrug and be like, 'Oh, it looks like no one's RSVPing, guess we'll just cancel the whole thing'?"

I swallowed hard, trying to hide the wobble I knew would be in my voice. "If I hide the invitations, and my parents realize nobody's RSVPing, they'll think nobody wants to come, and they won't want to tell me that and hurt my feelings. And you forgot the—"

"I didn't forget the part where you were going to pretend to be your mom and cancel the venue." Zoe crossed her arms and raised an eyebrow at me. We might not otherwise have looked anything alike, but we *were* eyebrow twins. "You seriously think the country club people are going to think you're an adult on the phone?"

A shudder rippled through me, and not only because the air-conditioning vent directly above me had just kicked on with a *whoosh* of frigid air. "Me, use the *phone*?" I shook my head as hard as I could. "That's what email is for."

Zoe raised her other eyebrow. "No. No way."

"What's wrong with email?"

"Don't be *obtuse*."

I raised my eyes at her for using the word *obtuse*. Zoe used it all the time with her weiner dog, Dogzilla. *Don't be* obtuse, *you definitely know what* get down from the table *means. Don't be* obtuse, *you know you're not supposed to have your head in the garbage can.*

It was a nicer way of saying *stupid*. Which I was definitely not. I turned my head so she couldn't see the hurt on my face, staring instead at the display of banned books decorating the wall.

Zoe continued, "It's *obviously* not about the email. It's

this entire plan." She smoothed her hand over her black braids. "No. No way."

"It's not like I'm asking you to steal a car," I said. She gave me a dubious look, like she thought that was coming next. "Zoe! You don't have to do anything that'll get your hands dirty. I just need you to be my lookout."

"Hello, girls!" The voice made us both jump. We turned to find a woman beaming down at us with a mouthful of bright white teeth. She was definitely older than Hannah—maybe in college or something?—and had light brown skin stretched too tight over her face by her high ponytail. "You must be Zoe and Ellie!"

I nodded, trying to turn my lips up into a smile. Fortunately I had Zoe there, so I didn't actually have to say anything. "I'm Zoe, and she's Ellie," Zoe said, pointing at me with her thumb.

"Wonderful!" It was like everything that came out of this woman's mouth ended in an exclamation point. I was exhausted just listening to her. "I'm Andrea Santos, and I'm the volunteer coordinator here at the library! I'm so excited to have you here with us!"

"We're so excited to be here, too," Zoe said flatly.

Andrea didn't seem to notice how unexcited Zoe

sounded. She just clapped her hands together. "Fantastic! Let me take you back to the meeting room! You'll be setting up for the crafts session you'll be running!"

I froze. *Crafts session? That we'll be running?*

That didn't sound like shelving books.

Still, I followed along as Andrea led Zoe and me through the children's section. We stepped over fluffy stuffed animals strewn all over the carpet, but those obstacles were nowhere near as dangerous as the little kids running and hollering in the aisles of colorful picture books and toys. Weren't libraries supposed to be quiet?

The meeting room was just an empty room with a dirty floor and a long table in the middle. The lone window looked out behind the library, where sports fields stretched into the distance. I turned back to the table just in time for Andrea to give us our instructions, punctuated (!) with (!) lots (!) of (!) enthusiasm (!), tell us to find her with any questions, and beat it.

I wasn't sure why we needed so many instructions— all we were doing was cutting out shapes from construction paper with blunt-edged safety scissors. We sat down and got started. "What did she mean, we were going to be running this crafts thing?" I asked Zoe.

She wasn't having it. "You said you wanted me to be a lookout for your absurd plan," she said, sawing through the paper with determination. "When someone commits a crime, the lookout also goes to jail. Because they were just as much a part of it." She sighed. "I was nervous when I got confirmed in the church, too. I had to get up in front of the whole congregation and everything. Remember?"

Of course I remembered. But she'd been one of many people getting confirmed at once, and she didn't have to do anything even close to singing an entire opera in front of the congregation. Not that I'd be singing an entire opera, either, but sometimes that's what the idea of singing my haftorah and Torah portions felt like, since they were in a language I didn't understand, to a strict, well-defined tune, and in front of an enormous crowd of people.

Plus, even if Zoe had been nervous, she got, like, normal person nervous, not nervous like me. She didn't have that fire still burning inside her like I did. Staying quiet and ducking my head kept it burning low, but I always knew it was there.

She would never understand. All it would take was a fan of the flames—lots of eyes on me, or someone asking me to stand up—and it would roar back to life. *She* hadn't been inside my body while it was gasping for breath and sweating out all the liquid inside. *She* hadn't been there in social studies a few months after Hannah's bat mitzvah, when I had to get up in front of the class and I forgot my speech with all those eyes on me and I started sweating and shaking and feeling like I was going to pass out . . . or a few months after that, when all the girls I usually sat with at lunch were absent and I had to find somewhere new to sit and the flames roared up inside me and tried to burn me alive.

I literally could have died.

"There's nothing you could say to convince me," Zoe said. "Nothing. I've made my decision."

Well. That sounded like a challenge to me.

I cocked my head and studied my best friend like I'd never seen her before. What did she love?

The answer came to mind right away: Dogzilla. Everything was clear now. All I had to do was kidnap Dogzilla and she'd do whatever I said.

No. Ellie Katz, you are not a dognapper.

But maybe there was *some* merit to that line of thinking. Not the life of crime part; the animal part. Because Zoe didn't just love animals, she loooooooved them. Like, she used to be one of those girls who are totally obsessed with horses, even though she'd never actually ridden one. She had a full set of those chapter books about girls who rode horses together, and she always wore her hair in a ponytail because it had *pony* in the name. And she'd tickle me to death if I ever told anyone about it, but when we were younger, she pretended one of those sticks with a stuffed horse head on the end was a real horse. She "fed" it carrots and everything.

Stick-horse was buried somewhere in the back of her closet, but Zoe still liked to wear one of those cat-ear headbands. And she liked to dress Dogzilla up in her old clothes. (That dachshund could really pull off a dress.)

"B'nai mitzvah cost a lot of money," I said. She stared at me, her face unreadable, but we both knew it. We'd overheard my parents talking about it. "But why spend all that money on a big party when we could put it to better use?"

"Like what?" She was frowning at me now, but she was also leaning in toward me. She was interested, which was a good sign.

Of course, Andrea chose that moment to pop her head in the door. "Hey, guys!" she chirped. "The kids are almost ready! Are you?"

"We're almost done," Zoe said.

Andrea popped back out, leaving my stomach to bubble. What happened to shelving books quietly all day? Now I had to deal with a bunch of sticky kids pasting things together? This wasn't what I'd signed up for.

But I had more important things to worry about. I almost had Zoe on the hook. "How about the animal rescue?" I said. She perked up immediately, so I kept going. "Every bat mitzvah has a charity project attached, usually to collect money or items for some topic the kid is passionate about."

"I know." Of course, I already knew she knew. She told me once she wished she had a bat mitzvah so she could run a drive for the animal rescue nearby where she'd found Dogzilla years ago. She could still try to do a charity drive, but money was a traditional gift for b'nai mitzvah.

Time for the clincher. I pulled myself up, angling my face so that I seemed to be looking down at her . . . even though she was at least four inches taller than me. "If I manage to get this bat mitzvah canceled . . . I bet some of those funds could be shifted to the animal rescue." A beat of silence. Another beat. I held her gaze, trying to look like I had any authority at all to "shift" my parents' "funds."

Maybe I would've been good at drama club after all.

Unfortunately the effect of my great acting was ruined, because just then the door flew open and a pack of kids poured inside. Little kids. Like, kindergartners. And somehow they were all shouting.

Zoe nudged me on the shoulder. "Ellie," she hissed. "I'm pretty sure that one little kid is Danny Cohen's brother."

I fought back a sigh. Zoe'd had a crush on Danny Cohen all year. She sat behind him in math and science, and liked to beg me for intel from our Hebrew school classes together. I almost never had anything interesting to tell her. He spent most of our Hebrew school classes sitting in the back of the room with his friends, laughing every time someone's chair made a fart noise.

This little kid did look vaguely like Danny Cohen, though all little kids looked kind of alike to me. "How do you know?"

"I saw them together at his soccer practice."

"Since when do you play soccer?"

"Since I snuck out of my study group to go watch Danny Cohen play," Zoe said. She smiled at my gawk-mouthed expression, then turned to the teeming mass of little kids and clapped her hands. "Okay, everybody! Listen close, because I'm not going to repeat myself!"

She did repeat herself. Three times. But eventually she got the little kids arranged around the tables with glue sticks and paper to work on their crafts. She walked around each table, cooing over the kids' projects when they held them up to her and answering their questions, while I wandered around the room trying to look approachable enough for Andrea not to get upset if she walked in but not approachable enough for any of the kids to actually ask me for help.

After ten minutes or so, most of the kids were quietly absorbed in either making their crafts or peeling dried glue off their skin, so Zoe walked over to me. "I thought about your proposal," she whispered out of the side of her mouth.

I knew she was talking about me asking her to be my lookout for my foolproof, one-hundred-percent-perfect, no-way-it-can-fail bat mitzvah sabotage, but I couldn't resist the obvious joke. "So are you going to marry me?"

She frowned. "This is serious." She sighed. It was a gusty sigh, the kind she sighed before giving in. "I'll do it.

But I'll *only* be your lookout, and I'm *only* doing it for the animals."

"Woof, woof," I replied. When she squinted at me with confusion, I translated. "Those were the dogs saying thank you."

A grin flashed over her face. "*Mroooow.* Those were the cats saying you're welcome." Then vanished. "And that I'd better not get my phone taken away for this."

"Don't worry," I said. "After all, like I said, this plan is absolutely foolproof, one-hundred-percent-perfect, no-way-it— *MMPH!*"

For someone so worried about getting her phone taken away and/or going to jail, Zoe was awfully casual about attacking me in front of a room of witnesses.

CHAPTER 4

There are a lot of good things about summer, but one of the best is that my dad's always home in the mornings. He's a teacher at the high school, so we have all the same breaks. As Zoe and I padded into the kitchen in our pajamas, he turned to us with a big grin on his face and a spatula in his hand. "It's about time you guys got up," he said. "Did you get *tired* of *sleeping*?"

I rolled my eyes as he burst out laughing. Why was it the best that my dad was home during the summer? It certainly wasn't because of the corny dad jokes he stored up the whole school year.

But the smell drifting over toward us from the stove? That tantalizing dance of the caramelized bananas, homemade candied pecans, and frying challah bread soaked in egg wash and sugar?

I'd roll my eyes through a thousand dad jokes for one slice of that French toast. Zoe told me she wanted to sleep over after our first library volunteering week to celebrate, but I knew it was really about breakfast. And the fact that we got to stay up all night giggling at videos of cats sitting in chairs like people and creeping on our classmates' social media without getting yelled at.

"Morning," Zoe said as we took seats at the table. "Where's Hannah? Still sleeping?"

"That's what happens when you become a teenager, girls," he said, turning around with a mock stern expression on his face. "Even French toast isn't enough to get you out of bed."

As Zoe began to debate with him that she was *almost* a teenager and she'd *still* followed the scent trail of the French toast downstairs the way Dogzilla followed the scent trail of her brother's dirty socks dropped around the house, I began to zone out. I *was* still kind of tired, but I wasn't sure if that's because I was almost a teenager or because Zoe had kept me up half the night tossing and turning and hitting me with her very sharp elbows.

I could live with that, though. The only reason I survived our first week of library volunteering was because of her. I was basically her silent shadow as she told kids how to do crafts, read them stories, and helped them and their parents pick out books. So I owed her all the French toast she could eat.

Speaking of Zoe's sharp elbows, one hit me in the side right now. I jumped in my seat to find both Zoe and my dad looking curiously at me. Clearly I'd missed a question or something. "I was just asking Uncle Nat about your bat mitzvah plans," Zoe said, her eyes going cartoonishly wide, her lips making exaggerated movements with every word.

Maybe I didn't want her to be my lookout after all. She was the *worst* liar.

But it wasn't like I had anyone else to ask. As it turns out, keeping to yourself and not doing any activities and not talking in front of people didn't exactly lead to having a lot of friends at school. Or Hebrew school. At least at school I had Zoe.

Of course, there was Hannah. But if I asked Hannah for help, I'd somehow come out of this whole thing with even more guests at my bat mitzvah than I'd started with.

Fortunately Dad was looking at me, so he didn't notice Zoe being ridiculous. "Are you excited, Ells?" he asked. "I know I am! I'm ready for that father-daughter dance."

I forced my lips to turn up at the edges, but I was positive my eyes were wild with panic.

"But, Nat," Zoe said, still emphasizing every single word. "Maybe you and Ellie should *talk* about what she *wants*."

My dad's eyes crinkled at the corners as he piled some French toast on a plate, then drowned it in bananas, sprinkled it with nuts, and slid it over to me. I grabbed a fork. "We already talked about it at our family meeting, right? Anything you want to add, Ells?"

His eyes were still kind, but now they bored into me. The fire jumped inside me, making sweat pop out on my forehead. He thought everything was fine, but really it wasn't. If I did what Zoe wanted, I'd be telling him something he didn't want to hear. Something that would make him look at me differently. My breath caught in my throat. I could just imagine those eyebrows crinkling in disappointment. *Really, Ellie? After we paid all this money? You can't even handle what Hannah did? I thought you were better than that.*

My heart beat like a rabbit's. "Ells?" my dad prompted. I stared down at the French toast on my plate. The French toast! Hannah's fiery cake had been my undoing, but *this* pastry could save me by buying me more time. Pastry redemption! I grabbed my fork and stuffed an enormous bite in my mouth.

And promptly choked. This was it, then. This was how I would die.

Eliana Rachel Katz, age twelve, choked to death Wednesday morning on a bite of banana-pecan French toast, with her father and best friend at her side. Her best friend cried, "I shouldn't have forced her into an awkward conversation! Really, this is all my fault." Her father said, "I don't understand how this could have happened. Her older sister, Hannah, makes eating French toast look fun and easy." Because "nobody wastes food in this house" (a quote from the deceased's mother), witnesses wrapped

up the remainder of the deceased's
French toast and stored it carefully
in the fridge for tomorrow's breakfast.

"Ells?" My dad slid a glass of water over toward me.
"Here, take a drink."

In between the coughs, I grabbed the glass and gulped
down a few sips. The blockage in my throat slid down to
my stomach in one solid, uncomfortable lump. I swallowed again to test my throat. It was sore.

"What were you saying before you almost keeled over,
Ellie?" Zoe prompted. Her eyes were boring into me, too.
It was like she and my dad were having a contest to see
who could drill into my skull with their eyes. They were
both losing, because it was physically impossible to drill
through bone with eye beams, but they were trying really,
really hard.

I swallowed again. It came easier this time. "What
song did you have in mind for our dance?" I asked. Zoe
huffed a sigh, but I didn't look at her. I couldn't. This was
an impossible conversation, really. No matter what direction I went in, I'd be disappointing somebody.

And I'd rather disappoint Zoe than my parents.

Dad's eyes lit up with excitement. See? I'd done the right thing. He rattled off a bunch of songs I'd never heard of, but I nodded along, pretending like I knew them. And then he snapped his fingers. "That reminds me. Thanks for bringing your bat mitzvah up. Your invitations came in yesterday!"

"Oh, really?" I tried to sound casual, but inside my heart was racing again. This was it, then. Part one of the plan: Get rid of the invitations and make sure nobody realizes it until it's too late to send out more. If a tree falls in the forest, does it make a sound if no one's there to hear it? And if there's a bat mitzvah, is it really going to happen if nobody's there to see it?

Okay, Ellie. Sound normal. You can do this. "So, what's the plan? With the invitations? Who's going to mail them out and when?"

Dad blinked. "Those are some very specific questions," he said. I braced myself for the interrogation to follow, but he only shrugged. "I printed out some address labels for the guest list, so you'll have to apply them. Then whoever's around will drop them in the mailbox, I guess."

This was my chance. I popped up from my seat, the rest of my French toast forgotten. Which just goes to show you how big a deal this was. "Zoe and I can do the address labels now."

"Wow, I didn't have to threaten you or anything," he said lightly. "You must be really excited for your bat mitzvah!"

I swallowed. Somehow, this time, it hurt again. "Something like that."

"Well, I won't hold you back," Dad said. "If you and Zoe want to get started, they're all stacked together on Mom's desk."

I flashed him a thumbs-up. "Got it." I grabbed Zoe by the arm.

"I'm not done eating!" she protested. But I gave her arm a tug, and she stuffed one last bite in her mouth, then followed after me, grumbling the whole time. "When I agreed to this stupid plan of yours, I didn't know I'd have to sacrifice my *French toast*."

"Sssssshhh!" I hissed, looking around to make sure nobody had heard. "You can have more later."

"Sure, when it's all *cold* and *soggy* and *blah*."

I tuned Zoe out as we headed toward the office, which was really just a nook on the side of the living room where Mom had a desk. I didn't see why she needed a desk at home when she already had a perfectly good desk at work. Zoe and I passed by the squashy brown couch and the coffee table where I wasn't allowed to leave any papers or books or anything (which seemed unfair, since Mom's desk was covered in papers).

Today, a stack of those papers was my invitations. A big fat stack. I grabbed them, flipping through to make sure I had the right thing. Yep, these were the pink-and-silver invitations I'd selected from the big book of choices, with Mom and Dad proudly inviting over a hundred people to celebrate the bat mitzvah of Eliana Rachel Katz.

"Those are a lot of invitations," Zoe observed.

"Thanks, Captain Obvious." I scanned the desk for the address labels, then grabbed them all, too. Not that I'd be using any of them, but Mom and Dad would be awfully suspicious if I claimed that the invitations had been sent out to Uncle Barry and his wife and Cousin Jeff and his husband if Uncle Barry's and Cousin Jeff's addresses were still hanging out here on the desk. "Okay, I think we're good."

"Good is the exact opposite of what we are," Zoe muttered, but I ignored her and clutched the invitations to my chest as I dragged her back to my room. I heard Hannah groan for me to be quiet across the hall just before I slammed my door extra hard.

It was time for her to wake up anyway.

Safe in my room, I stuffed the invitations under my mattress. "There, that was easy," I said with satisfaction.

Zoe rolled her eyes. "Yeah, until it comes time to mail them out."

I tapped the side of her head. "I'm going to tell my dad that my mom took them, and my mom that my dad took them," I said. "Like I said. Easy."

I expected Zoe to grumble some more, but instead, she sighed with relief. "Good, I'm glad that's over, then."

I shook my head. "Over? Oh, it's not over." I smiled at her. "We're just getting started."

CHAPTER 5

As expected, my invitations plan went off without a hitch. The invitations and the labels got dusty under my mattress as I told Dad I'd given them all to Mom to drop into the mailbox, and vice versa. They just nodded distractedly at me and said thank you.

I told Zoe this when she came to sleep over after our second week at the library. Just like the first week, I'd spent it stuck to Zoe's side so that I didn't have to talk to anyone I didn't know. I even got to spend some time shelving books. It was wonderfully peaceful. "It's working so far, which just means we have to keep going," I said.

She sighed. "Fine. What's next?"

The invitations had been dealt with, but that didn't mean I was safe. My parents could still realize something was up: One of their temple friends could ask if their invitation had been lost in the mail, because they'd seen my bat mitzvah date on the schedule but hadn't received their invitation yet. Or my parents could start to wonder why they weren't getting any RSVPs. I might have cut one bat mitzvah branch off the tree, but I had to attack this thing at the roots. Like, pour some bleach on them so that the whole tree withered and died.

"This metaphor is going kind of far," Zoe said, sounding worried. "We're not actually cutting down a tree, right?"

Anyway. If my parents realized something had gone wrong with the invitations, they could still send out a mass text or email and do their best to assemble the Old Person Squad.

"But the Old Person Squad can't assemble if there's nowhere for them to go," I said with relish. The feeling of a plan well-done actually tasted a little bit like relish in my mouth, tangy and sweet. "So we're going to cancel the venue."

"Right." Zoe groaned, flopping down on my beanbag chair. It squished out around her like it was trying to absorb her into its depths. "You're going to hack into your mom's email."

The way she said it sent a nervous flutter through my insides. "It's not really *hacking*," I said. "I know my mom's password. It's just *hannahellie*. She uses it for everything."

"That's a terrible password. It doesn't even have any numbers."

"I know."

"If you have the password, couldn't we just log into it at my house?" Zoe asked. "Then you don't have to worry about her catching you."

I shook my head grimly. "I wish," I said. "But what if she happened to log in at the same time I was typing out the email to the venue? I'd get caught right away. No, I have to do it here, at home, while you're keeping an eye out, so that I know we'll be safe."

"Do it on your phone," Zoe said. "Then we can just pretend we're doing whatever, and I wouldn't even have to be a lookout."

I shook my head even more grimly. "I don't have the email app on my phone, since I don't have an email, and my parents have a block on downloading new apps. So it *has* to be on my mom's laptop."

"It's like your mom is making this difficult on purpose," Zoe mumbled.

"Well, she kind of is," I said. "It's not like she *wants* us to do this."

Zoe mumbled the next thing even more quietly, so that I couldn't quite hear, but it sounded a lot like *Neither do I.*

"Woof, woof," I barked. She glared at me. I grinned back, exposing my sharp canines. Canines as in dogs. Get it?

She did not. She drew back. "You look like you're going to eat me."

"I promise I won't," I said, but she didn't look any less weirded out.

Just then, the whine of a lawn mower drifted in from outside the window. I sat bolt upright in bed. "That would be Mom mowing the lawn," I said. She liked doing it for some reason, something about being surrounded by the smell of freshly cut grass. And it was literally the perfect time to go into her email, because she wouldn't stop mowing the lawn in the middle. If for some reason she did, we'd hear the lawn mower switch off and have time to escape before she came inside. "If we're lucky, Dad'll be out running errands. That means your job is just to make sure Mom doesn't come into the office!"

I tried to make it sound like I was telling her that her new bedtime was midnight, but she wasn't buying it. "You're lucky I'm such a good friend," she informed me, and I nodded, because even though she was being all grumbly, I *was* lucky to have her in my life. I didn't know what I'd do without her.

And not just with my foolproof, one-hundred-percent-perfect, no-way-it-can-fail plan. With life in general. Like at the library, making sure I didn't have to do anything I wasn't comfortable with. Or at school. Sure, there were girls I sat with in the cafeteria when Zoe and I didn't have the same lunchtime and other girls I partnered with for group projects when Zoe and I weren't in the same class, but I didn't really talk to them. Definitely not the way I talked to Zoe. I drew her in for a quick, tight hug, which pulled a *squawwwk* out of her. "Very birdlike," I told her. She beamed, taking it as a compliment. "Now let's go."

We exited my room, and walked straight into . . .

. . . Hannah. "Good morning," she said. Her eyes raked over me. I flushed, because I knew she was totally judging me for still wearing those patterned matching pajama tops and bottoms Nana got us for Chanukah every year instead of an old T-shirt and men's boxers, which was what she and her friends had deemed the acceptable kind of pajamas.

I really didn't need her here right now. Especially not with our plan so time-sensitive and ready to go. I jutted out my chin. "Good morning. Um, going somewhere?"

"Where would I be going?" She sounded surprised.

Which was ridiculous, because she was literally *always* going somewhere. Hannah could never just be by herself. She had an ever-growing and changing list of best friends. If she wasn't out at one of her (many) activities, she was at a friend's house or an acquaintance's house or, I don't know, probably a stranger's house. Which would usually be dangerous, but with Hannah's laugh and charm and talkative personality, they wouldn't be a stranger by the end of the day.

But I couldn't say all that. Especially not right now when Zoe and I were on a time limit; we had to be done with all this by the time my mom finished mowing the lawn. She wouldn't mow the lawn again for another couple of weeks. Why did grass have to grow *so* slowly?

I shrugged. "I dunno," I said.

Hannah stepped forward with a big smile. I didn't think I'd ever smiled that big—I wasn't sure if my mouth was even capable of opening that wide. It gleamed, like she was actually part of a toothpaste commercial. That would explain a lot, really. *Mr. and Mrs. Katz, we've finished filming our commercial, and we have nowhere to leave this extremely photogenic orphan! Could you take her?*

"I was thinking we could hang out today." Hannah gestured behind me, at the photo board of us she'd made for me. "Maybe add some new pictures to that wall!"

Why today? Why at all? "What, are none of your real friends around?" The words escaped me before I could help myself. They sounded kind of mean, and I regretted them as soon as I saw Hannah's big smile falter.

"You *are* my real friend." She took another step toward me, and I could smell the minty freshness of her breath. "Maybe we can . . . I don't know . . . USY is having a day where they're taking people to the local parks and playgrounds to do cleanup. I was thinking about going if you were busy, but maybe you could come with me! I know you're still in Kadima, but I bet they'd let you come along!"

USY was the Jewish youth group for high schoolers, and Kadima was the middle school version. I'd been in Kadima all year, but I didn't go to very many activities. There were lots of dances and conventions and other social events, but without Zoe, the thought of going to one of those things made me shrivel up in horror. No matter how many times Zoe told me I should go. She belonged to a similar program through her church and didn't seem to understand that sleeping over at a stranger's house for a weekend or spending a week in a cabin with other strangers was basically my worst nightmare.

Naturally, in eighth grade, Hannah had been president of her Kadima chapter.

Even if I didn't already have (foolproof, one-hundred-percent-perfect, no-way-they-can-fail) plans today, the absolute last thing I'd want to do would be hanging out in a park with a bunch of strange high schoolers, picking up garbage all day. I'd rather go to the dentist. Or quietly shelve library books.

"I can't today," I said, my eyes straying past her down the hallway. *Come on, Hannah. Move.* "We have stuff to do."

"We?"

Zoe popped her head over my shoulder. "Hi, Hannah!" I didn't have to look at her to know that her eyes were sparkling. She loved Hannah, for some reason. She'd told me more than once that she wished she had a big sister like Hannah instead of a stupid little brother. *You can take her*, I'd say. Zoe wouldn't laugh.

"Hey, Zoe!" Hannah smiled over my shoulder. "How's Dogzilla doing?"

"He ate an entire jar of jelly beans the other night, so he had fluorescent rainbow poop for a whole day," Zoe said.

"That sounds gross and awesome," Hannah said. "How about Danny Cohen?"

How did Hannah know Zoe liked Danny Cohen? And when had they discussed it? I scowled at the wall as Zoe stammered a nonresponse, deciding that, during our next library session, I'd figure out some way to use Danny's little brother to help Zoe get to him. I could make more than one foolproof plan at once. I'd show her that she didn't need Hannah's help, just like I didn't need it.

"We'd better keep going," I said, interrupting their chatter.

Hannah's eyes zeroed in on me. My heart jumped into my throat. For a moment, I felt like she could see through the bone of my skull right into my brain. Like I was a marquee, and she could read all my scrolling neon thoughts.

And then her lips turned back up at the ends. Funny, I hadn't even noticed her stop smiling. "Okay, well, have fun doing, um, whatever you're doing," she said. "I guess I'll go clean up garbage with Sarah."

"Thanks," I said. "Have fun with all the garbage."

Her door closed before she could respond.

CHAPTER 6

With both Hannah and my mom out of the way and Dad somewhere that wasn't here, the path to the laptop was clear. I plopped down in Mom's plush leather office chair, warm air from the open window drifting over me with the smell of fresh-cut grass. "You hang out in the hallway and stall anyone who looks like they might come in here," I directed Zoe. "And warn me if you can't. Like, talk really loud so that I can hear you or something."

"Maybe we should figure out a secret signal." She perked up. "Oh! Maybe I should bark like a dog! Or caw like a bird!"

"I don't know, that sounds pretty obvious," I said. She wilted. "Just . . . figure it out as it goes. We can do this!"

Zoe gave me a determined nod and bounced out of

the room, shutting the door behind her. That left me in silence, with nothing but the buzzing of the lawn mower in the background to break my concentration.

"All right," I whispered to myself. I was so focused I didn't even feel nervous. "First: Get logged in and pick up the trail."

As it turned out, I didn't need Mom's password after all. I waved my finger on the trackpad to turn the screen saver off, and she was already logged in right there in front of me.

"Very convenient, if terrible for security," I said. Why were parents so bad with technology? Seriously, it took both Mom and Dad, like, ten minutes to type out a single text. "Now, to search for any emails with the venue . . ."

That was also an easy thing to find: All I had to do was type *Eagle Crest Manor*, the name of the country club, into the search bar, and a whole list of emails arranging the date, time, and details popped up. I ignored the ones from a few years ago, which were for Hannah's bat mitzvah, and focused on the most recent ones. Since we were still three months away, they hadn't corresponded about things like dropping off flowers or figuring out how the DJ was going to set up his equipment yet—they'd just confirmed that the bat mitzvah of Eliana Rachel Katz would be taking place on the evening of Saturday, September 26.

"Time to fix that," I muttered. I opened up a new response and began to type.

> Dear Ms. Winters,
> Unfortunately I need to cancel this bat mitzvah because

Ummm . . . what would be a reason to cancel a bat mitzvah that nobody could argue with, and that might be sympathetic enough to get our deposit back so we could give it to Zoe's animal rescue? It wasn't like I could say the bat mitzvah girl no longer wanted one. My parents wouldn't understand that, and I bet this woman wouldn't, either.

> Dear Ms. Winters,
> Unfortunately I need to cancel this bat mitzvah because Ellie died and you can't have a bat mitzvah if you're dead.

I smiled with satisfaction. Can't argue with deadness. I raised my hands and finished typing the email, the keys clacking loudly in the silence.

> So, we would like to cancel the venue
> and have our deposit back, please.
> Thank you.
> Sincerely,
> Liz Katz

I read it over quickly for typos, then hit send. There. "That was easy," I said. My words sounded extra loud in the quiet of the room. "Now I just need to delete it from the sent . . ."

I trailed off, because . . . Wait. The silence? The quiet of the room? What had happened to—

"OH, HEY, IT'S LIZ! LOOK AT YOU, BACK INSIDE FROM MOWING THE LAWN!" Zoe thundered from the hallway.

I said some very bad words under my breath.

"Zoe, good morning." I could hear my mom perfectly, despite her speaking at a normal volume. More very bad words. That had to mean she was right outside in the hallway. I quickly deleted my email from the sent folder; hopefully Ms. Winters wouldn't email her back and would just cancel the venue without following up.

How could I spin this? I took a deep, shaky breath. If only real life were like email, where I could carefully think about everything I was going to say and review it for anything that wasn't right. Things would be so much easier that way.

"GOOD MORNING, LIZ, WHERE ARE YOU GOING?" Somehow, Zoe was shouting even louder than before. "YOU LOOK LIKE YOU'RE GOING TOWARD YOUR OFFICE! YOUR OFFICE, WHERE YOUR COMPUTER IS!"

"Yes, that's the point." Mom sounded more amused than anything else, which was good, I guessed. "I'm waiting for an important email."

"OH, AN IMPORTANT EMAIL, SO YOU'RE GOING TO CHECK YOUR EMAIL IN THE OFFICE."

A beat of silence. "Zoe, could you please move just slightly to your left?"

Somehow my hand was sweating and freezing at the same time. I had to X out of my mom's email so that she wouldn't get suspicious. But she'd left it up, so if I closed out of it, maybe that would look even *more* suspicious. Maybe—

An email popped up from Ms. Winters. I could just see in the preview: *Liz, I'm so, so sorry to hear this. Of course we can—*

The doorknob squeaked as it turned. I didn't have the time to read the rest of it—I clicked delete as fast as I could, then switched over to the trash folder, hit delete again, and watched the email disappear into the ether.

The door opened. My face heated up, though I was looking away. Okay, I could do this. Okay, okay, just, what should I say, what was there to say—

"Oh, Ellie!" Mom sounded surprised. "What are you up to?"

I was twelve years old. I knew so many words. Why couldn't I think of any of them? Bamboozle. Palimpsest. Refrigerator. *No, none of those are useful right now!*

"Ellie?" Mom prompted. I couldn't even look at her, just stared right at the screen. At her email. I took a deep breath. Maybe I'd suck in some words from the screen.

A new email popped up. I gasped, and the gasp strangled in my throat. It had to be Ms. Winters. She was emailing about something she'd forgotten, and my mom would see exactly what I was up to, and—

```
Eliana Rachel Katz, age twelve, died
Sunday morning after she was screamed
at to death by her mother. Her older
sister said, "If Ellie had just come
with me to clean up garbage like a
normal person, her eardrums wouldn't
have exploded." Her best friend cried,
"I HAVE NO IDEA HOW THIS HAPPENED! I
AM TOTALLY INNOCENT!" At press time,
the    deceased's    mother    was    still
sitting atop the body in her computer
chair, because she had an important
email to respond to and it takes her
approximately eight years to type a
single sentence.
```

"Oh!" Mom exclaimed. This was it. This was how it would start. A normal volume first, then Zoe volume, then something that would shatter my ears and melt my brain and—

"Ellie, scoot." That didn't sound like yelling. I hopped to my feet, my shaky legs barely managing to hold me up, and my mom took my place, her eyes focused on the screen.

My eyes, blurry before, now focused. The email was from her boss. She clicked on it, and spreadsheets popped up on the screen.

"Do you need something?" she asked me, already squinting at the numbers. "Unless you want to sit here and watch me analyze these spreadsheets by five . . ."

"No! No, that's okay!" The words! The words were back! And my legs weren't shaking anymore! I sent an enthusiastic, silent thank-you to my mom's boss. Almost as if her boss were God or something.

This might get me tossed out of Hebrew school, but right now, I'd perform an entire Saturday morning service to my mom's boss.

Zoe was waiting out in the hallway, positively shaking with either fear or excitement, I had no idea. "Well?" she whispered. "How did it go?"

I glanced from side to side, then pulled her into the kitchen. "I think it went okay," I whispered back. "I sent the email and got an email back from the lady, which I deleted before my mom could see it."

"Did she cancel it?"

Liz, I'm so, so sorry to hear this. Of course we can . . .

"I think so," I said, trying to sound more confident than I felt. I mean, what else could that email have meant? She wouldn't say she was sorry that of course we can definitely not cancel the date and give you your money back.

"So they refunded the deposit for the animal rescue?" Zoe asked.

"I think so," I said again.

"So when can we—"

"We can't say anything to my parents until the date's passed," I said. Because once the official date of my bat mitzvah was done, it wasn't like you could just reschedule it. You couldn't change the day you were born. "After that, we'll go to them together and tell them what we want to do with the money."

"Okayyyy . . ." Zoe said, sounding about the least convinced a person could sound.

"It's going to be okay," I said. "Want to do a yoga video?"

Her eyes lit up. "Yes, please."

We got our beach towels and brought our phones out to the yard, where we cued up a video by our favorite online yoga instructor. With every minute of deep breathing and stretching, my confidence grew. Not about the yoga, because I wasn't very flexible (I couldn't even touch my toes, unlike Zoe, who could bend over all the way double). About my plan. This *had* to be enough to cancel my bat mitzvah. Sure, they could still make me do my haftorah at temple, but you couldn't exactly have a party if no one was invited *and* if you didn't have anywhere to put them if they showed up anyway. I felt sure of it.

And I was.

At least for the next few weeks . . .

CHAPTER 7

I sailed through the next few weeks like I was walking on clouds. Nay, bouncing on clouds! Because I was free. The bat mitzvah monster had been banished, and the kingdom could rejoice. And the kingdom did rejoice, if by kingdom you meant me. Even Hannah commented on how bizarrely smiley I was, which sent that smile dropping right off my face. Still, she couldn't take the feeling away.

And then the whispers started.

I began hearing scraps of them in the hallway outside my room, one of my parents whispering to the other as they left their bedroom in the morning.

. . . said he never received it . . .

. . . haven't gotten any RSVPs . . .

. . . ask the post office?

And then there was the eruption. *That* one actually woke me up. I cracked my door open, poking my head into the hallway. Hannah was already poking her own head out, a baffled expression in place of her usual smile.

Mom was yelling. *Yelling*. Like, really loud! "—TELLING ME THAT YOU NEVER MAILED THEM OUT?"

And Dad! Dad was yelling back! Which was unusual! "NO, YOU MAILED THEM!"

The yells quieted into furious whispers as Hannah turned that baffled expression on me. It made my skin crawl uncomfortably. "What's that about, you think?"

I shrugged. I knew it had to be unconvincing, because it felt like one shoulder went way higher than the other, so I tried to even it out, and then all I was doing was shimmying my shoulders as Hannah's baffled expression got even more baffled. "Um, I dunno."

Hannah stared toward their door for another few seconds. "Weird," she said finally. When it became clear that they weren't going to start yelling again, she retreated back into her room, closing the door.

I, however, stayed right where I was. Because of course I knew what they were talking—no, yelling—about. My bat mitzvah invitations. They'd been confused about why they weren't getting any responses these last few weeks, and one of my parents must have made an offhand comment to the other, like *You mailed them that Monday, right? What mailbox?* and the other parent must've been all like, *No, you mailed them*, and then everything just escalated from there.

Soon enough they'd realize that the invitations had seemingly vanished into thin air.

I retreated back to my bed and felt around under the mattress. "Ouch!" I hissed, drawing my hand back. A paper cut had sliced across the pad of my middle finger.

Well, I kind of deserved that.

And it only got worse from there. My parents asked me about the invitations, but I only shrugged, and fortunately they didn't push it further. They seemed more mystified than angry or upset, which made me feel kind of guilty, to be honest.

But not guilty enough to come clean.

"We're not going to have time to order and mail out more invitations," my dad said to my mom in the kitchen one day over their cups of coffee. I was lurking at the table, eating a bowl of cereal. With all the stress, there hadn't been the time or mood for morning French toast. "We're going to have to send out an email blast or something." He shook his head. "Not exactly elegant, but it'll get the job done."

"If we have to," Mom said in response, scrolling through her phone. Her brows furrowed. "What's this big deposit in our account? Were we expecting some payment? For . . ." She named an amount of money that made my jaw drop.

"I don't think so," Dad said. "That doesn't sound like either of our paychecks. Who's it from?"

Mom was already scrolling down. "From Eagle Crest . . . with our sympathies? What?"

I tensed up in my seat. My bowl clattered on the table. I was sure they'd look over at me, but they were too caught up in the mysterious deposit.

"That's the country club. Ells's bat mitzvah venue," Dad said. "But why would they be refunding our money?"

"I have no idea," Mom replied. "I'll give them a call."

I stared into my bowl of cereal like it was actually a TV screen showing me something fascinating. It was either that or watch Mom as she held her increasingly loud conversation with the venue. "What are you talking about? We didn't cancel the bat mitzvah! . . . No! Wait, what? *Dead?* That's horrible, who would do that? . . . No! What do you mean, you already booked somebody else on that day? What about Sunday? . . . That whole weekend?"

"That didn't sound good," Dad said grimly. I assumed that meant Mom had hung up the phone, but there was no way I was going to look up from my cereal bowl turned TV screen to check.

She summarized the whole story to him, one that I, of course, already knew. "I just don't understand," she said. No, it was more like she wheezed. I peeked up in surprise. Her face was bright red, her eyes were shiny, and her lips were pressed together like she was trying not to throw up.

She looked almost . . . almost like . . . me.

"I just don't understand," she repeated, her voice higher and more strained this time. "Is somebody playing some horrible joke on us? On . . ." I felt her gaze land on the back of my head. I ducked back to my bowl. "Why would somebody do this?" She sucked in a deep breath. It sounded like she was trying to inhale through a really long straw. "What are we supposed to do now?"

Dad laid a hand on her shoulder. I could hear the thump all the way across the room, but it wasn't a mean sort of thump. It was more of a comforting thump, like Mom was about to float away and Dad was trying to hold her down.

"Breathe, Liz," he told her. "Just stop for a moment and take a few deep breaths."

Mom closed her eyes and took in a deep breath. It was shaky, like mine often were, but the next one was less so. By the third, it sounded almost normal. By the fourth, her eyes were open. By the fifth, her voice was steady again, sounding like its usual self.

"Okay," she said. "Unless we want to hire a lawyer, it sounds like the venue is gone. They already booked our weekend. And this close to the bat mitzvah date, we're not going to find another space at a good price. So either we pay out the ears or we have the party in the backyard."

"Maybe that wouldn't be so bad," Dad mused. "It would have to be a smaller party in the backyard, but since the invitations haven't been sent out yet, we don't have to worry about disinviting anyone. We can still have the people who matter." I held my breath with anticipation. Could this really be happening? "And the venue couldn't be any cheaper than free!"

I laughed loudly at his bad dad joke to encourage him. His eyebrows lifted, which meant either that he was absolutely encouraged or that my fake laugh sounded like I was choking and he was concerned.

"Think of what everyone at temple will say," Mom replied.

Dad shrugged. "Who cares? Aren't we always telling our daughters not to care about what people think?" He cracked a smile. "If anything, it might be nice to have a few less nosy old folks at our party."

"Hmmm."

I held back a smile. It seemed like my plan was actually working beyond my wildest dreams. A party in the backyard sounded *great*. I'd know the setting really well, and like my dad said, we could only fit so many people back there, so only close family and friends would be able to come. I couldn't believe it, but it sounded like my bat mitzvah could actually be . . . fun.

"And we could go with more casual catering for the more casual venue," Dad persuaded. "Remember the wedding we went to in your friend's backyard? We could get a kosher pizza oven! And an ice cream truck could come for dessert!"

"A pizza oven does sound good," Mom said. "But it doesn't matter what *we* think. It's about what Ellie thinks. After all, someone did this to . . ."

She trailed off, and I realized what she thought. She thought someone had done this to me. Like a bully in a movie, one who hated me so much they tried to dunk my head in a toilet and spread rumors that they'd seen me picking my nose and eating it. Saying I was dead to ruin my bat mitzvah was just another one of their sinister plans to ruin my life.

And from the look on my mom's face, I knew it was breaking her heart. Which made the guilt weigh me down again, heavy on my shoulders. I wasn't bullied at school or anything; mostly kids just acted like I didn't exist, since I was so quiet.

Maybe I *should* just have talked to my parents about how I felt. Would that have made the guilt go away?

Or would it have made the guilt turn into something else that wrapped its hands around my throat and squeezed as hard as it could, making the flames roar up inside me? Because I knew my parents would be confused and disappointed, and I couldn't handle that thought. Better that they pitied me. At least for now.

I shrank inward and tried to look as pathetic as possible. "I guess it's okay," I said. My parents still looked sad, which was bad. I made myself perk up a little bit. "A pizza oven and an ice cream truck would be pretty awesome."

"You know, okay," Mom said. She almost sounded happy. "Okay, we're really doing this. Big bat mitzvah off, backyard bat mitzvah on!" Actually happy now. "Wherever it ends up, we just have to let the DJ know. And cancel the caterer with enough time to get our deposit back."

My parents left the room for the office, talking logistics and numbers and other boring things as they sat down at the laptop. I took a celebratory slurp of cereal. *Backyard bat mitzvah.* I could get used to the sound of a backyard bat mitzvah. It sounded like victory.

And it was. We shrank down the guest list—sorry, Uncle Barry—and kept things small so I didn't freak out during my haftorah because there weren't too many eyes on me, and the pizza oven was just as amazing as I thought it would be, and nobody ever found out what I did, and we all lived happily ever after.

Just kidding.

Because Hannah's superpower was activating. The

same superpower that told her our family bat mitzvah meeting was happening. That extra sense that told her it was time to go stick her nose in something that didn't involve her.

So I knew that as I heard her stampede into the office after Mom and Dad that her nose must have been wriggling overtime. "Wait!" she hissed, but if she was trying to be quiet, her footsteps said the exact opposite.

What was she doing? I crept over toward the hallway, pressing my ear up against the living room door.

"What are you thinking?" Hannah said.

"Tone, young lady," Dad answered.

Hannah sighed heavily. "Fine. What are you thinking?" It didn't sound any different to me, but maybe her face had changed or something. "You're going to make Ellie have her bat mitzvah in the backyard?"

"It's the best option, it seems," said Mom. "And Ellie is on board."

"Yeah, because she didn't want to hurt your feelings," Hannah argued.

Oh my God. She really had no idea what she was talking about.

Hannah continued, "The poor kid has no friends and

now someone's sabotaged her party. If anyone needs a big party, it's her."

"She has a friend," Dad said, but he sounded uncertain. That couldn't be his feeling about the friend thing—Zoe and I were unquestionably tight—which meant he had to be uncertain about the party thing. No! I could see the pizza oven evaporating before my very eyes.

"If you do this to her, you might as well just tell her that she doesn't matter," Hannah said. I couldn't see her face, but I imagined her looking smug. Why else would she do this? As the effortlessly social big sister with a million friends, hadn't she made things hard *enough* for me by giving me an example I could never, ever live up to? "And you're telling whoever did this horrible thing to her that they win. Any bullying will just get worse for her after that."

Hannah paused dramatically to suck in a deep breath. "If anything, I think we need to make this party even bigger and better," she said. My mouth dropped open, and my palms started to sweat. Nooooo! Anything but that! "We need to show Ellie that she's really special and important, no matter what the other kids might do or say. We need to celebrate her!"

I held my breath as my parents debated, their tones too soft for me to hear through the door. "You know," Dad said finally. His tone was thoughtful, which made my stomach plummet. "You're right."

"I bet that the firehouse would be available," Mom said. "We have a connection, since your brother works there, Nat. And we could actually fit more people there than at the country club!"

I wheezed. This was the worst possible outcome. How could they do this to me?

Eliana Rachel Katz, age twelve, passed away Wednesday afternoon due to the sheer crushing weight of disappointment. "That poor girl, she must have been so disappointed that her original bat mitzvah plans were foiled," said her mother, crying. Her sister, Hannah, added, "We'll just have to host the biggest, best funeral." The family decided to turn Ellie's upcoming bat mitzvah party into a second bat mitzvah for Hannah.

"Perfect!" Hannah said. "Now, let me see your plans. I am going to help make this the *best bat mitzvah ever.*"

I backed away before I could hear any more. My heart was pounding hard, like it was trying to break out of my rib cage. I thought I might be sick. *More* people? At the *firehouse*, the social hall at the center of town that could fit *hundreds* of them? All of them dancing to music and staring at me and judging me and thinking—

I had to sit down. My butt thumped back into my kitchen chair. Cereal floated unappetizingly in the warm milk left before me. Everything had backfired. Was this it? Could I really give up on my plan and do this?

No. My mental response was so strong that I actually jumped in my seat. I couldn't give up now. There was no way I could handle a party at the firehouse. But I bet this time, Mom and Dad would be a lot more careful about what they told the venue. *Somebody pretended to be us to cancel our last venue. Don't cancel this bat mitzvah unless you have a retinal scan and fingerprints from both of us.*

And the invitations thing? The ship for that had sailed, too. I couldn't exactly hide the emails or texts Mom and Dad were going to send out, and again, they'd probably be a lot more careful with these than they'd been with the last round of invitations.

Which meant I had to get in this even deeper. The flames in me flared hot at the very thought. Could I really do this without burning up?

I had to. There was no other option.

CHAPTER 8

As expected, Mom and Dad booked the firehouse no problem, and they sent out the email invitations with confidence. A hundred and fifty invitations, to be exact, instead of their original hundred. The firehouse was a cheaper venue, so they were fine paying for more food from the caterer. Which meant they could pack in *all* the distant cousins and nosy temple biddies.

Anything to make their daughter feel better.

I wanted the backyard with the pizza oven and the ice cream truck—now that Dad had put the idea in my head, I couldn't get it out. But my parents and Hannah had plowed ahead. They hadn't even asked me what I wanted.

Not that I would've told them the truth if they had, I guess.

"So everything is terrible," I told Zoe as we walked into the library.

"Your plans totally backfired," Zoe said. I frowned. That wasn't the kind of support I was looking for. "Maybe you should just stop now before your parents rent out a baseball stadium and make you read your haftorah on a Jumbotron."

"They could never do that," I said. Right?

Right. "So we have to soldier on," I said. "I know the DJ isn't the most important part of the bat mitzvah, but he's supposed to come over tonight to talk about music choices and games and prizes and all that stuff. So we have to figure out how to . . . I don't know, make *him* cancel on *us*."

We didn't even have to stop at the library's info desk anymore to check in. All the librarians knew us. Well, they knew Zoe, and they knew what I looked like, which was close enough. The reference librarian smiled and waved at us as we walked back toward the children's section. "Hi, girls!"

"Hi, Ms. Coughlan!" Zoe said back. I just smiled and waved. The librarians were familiar to me now, but still not actually-say-words-to-them familiar.

Back through the teen hangout section, where we'd be allowed once we turned thirteen, and into the children's section. As usual, we were greeted by the sounds of hollering children and a hollering Andrea. "Good morning, girls!" she cried, bouncing to a stop in front of us. "Why don't you go pick out some picture books for storytime?!"

We nodded and decamped to the picture book section, kneeling side by side to look through the colorful spines. I'd grown to enjoy storytime a lot more than I thought I would. Zoe always read our selections to the little kids while I sat in the back, making sure they didn't act up too much. They never did. Zoe's voice somehow kept them spellbound. Them, and me. She was really good at acting the stories out as dramatically as possible. Probably from those years in elementary school when she had me video her singing in hopes that she'd go viral and make a billion dollars.

Once we had our choices, we sat down in the aisle, our backs up against the shelves of books, our feet up against another. "I saw Danny Cohen's brother when we walked in," Zoe whispered. "Probably waiting for storytime. Do you think Danny might come in to pick him up?"

"I dunno," I whispered back. "I think probably his parents are going to pick him up."

Zoe rolled her eyes. "Well, duh. I meant, maybe Danny might come *with* them."

"Maybe." It didn't hurt to give her a little bit of hope. "But what about the DJ? How are we going to make him cancel?"

Zoe bit her lip. "We could dump a bucket of ice water on him. That's how my brother got kicked out of Sunday school."

"Your brother dumped ice water on his Sunday school teacher?"

"No, on the priest," Zoe said, which definitely sounded worse. And like something I'd never be able to do. The whole room would be staring at me, and my parents would know immediately something was up. I told her that, and she looked up at the ceiling in thought. "Um, how about we just make your bat mitzvah sound awful? Like, tell him that you get cold easily, so the room's going to be a hundred degrees, and that the kids there are really obnoxious and won't stop screaming, and that every adult who goes has to get, like, five flu shots."

I shook my head. "My parents are going to be at this

meeting. They'd set the record straight. We can't be too obvious."

We sat there in silence for a moment, thinking about an under-the-radar way we could make the DJ hate us. And then it hit me. By *it*, I mean a board book thrown by a little kid that smacked me on the shoulder but also the perfect idea.

"I got it," I said once Zoe and I had retreated out of range of the little kid's throwing arm. "The meeting's about what we want him to play at my bat mitzvah, right? So we need to request things that he would never be able to play. He'll be forced to give up."

Zoe's eyes lit up. "Yesssssss. Like police sirens. And talk radio. And boring classical music."

"We'll work on it," I told her as Andrea came bustling over. Zoe held up the picture books we'd selected for storytime—a book about a pigeon driving a bus and another about a girl who befriends a squash—and Andrea nodded in approval.

"Excellent choices!" she told us. "Please go get the beanbags and chairs set up!"

Storytime was held in the corner of the children's section, which meant we had to clear out a bunch of toys and discarded books to make room for cushions for the little kids and chairs for us and the parents. I picked up and set down without complaint, thinking about the most outlandish music or sound effects I'd ever heard.

This might actually be kind of fun.

"Oh my God," Zoe said. Her voice came out breathless. I looked up from my cushion arranging to find her staring toward the main area, her mouth hanging open. "Danny's here! He must have come by after soccer practice!"

I followed her rapt eyes. Sure enough, there was Danny Cohen perusing the display of sports books. "He's really sweaty," I said.

"*So* sweaty," Zoe gasped. "I'm going to go say hi, okay? Is that okay?"

"It's fine," I said. "I can finish up here."

Zoe didn't even say thank you, just took off for the main area at the same gallop she used to ride on her stick-horse, slowing to a reasonable speed once she got close. I saw her wipe her palms on her pants before stepping up beside him. She glanced sidelong at him as she looked through the sports books also, picking up one with a giant orange basketball on the cover. Zoe hated basketball, but she wasn't looking at it. She just kept looking over at Danny.

I wanted to scream, *Talk to him!* from across the room, but one, that would've been extremely weird, and two, who was I to tell her that when I never talked to anyone?

"Looks good!"

I jumped in surprise at Andrea's voice behind me, nearly falling over. "The kids are coming!" she continued. "Get ready!"

I couldn't possibly get ready. I just stared at Andrea, at an impasse. My heart started beating hard. The flames started licking at my insides. I couldn't do storytime with these kids. *Tell her that*, I told myself. *Tell her you have to get Zoe.*

But that would involve talking to Andrea and telling her something she definitely wouldn't want to hear. My tongue shriveled up in my mouth as she strode away, apparently confident her wishes were being carried out.

I glanced over at Zoe. She caught my eye. *Thank goodness.* I waved frantically for her to get over here. She frowned and looked over at Danny again, but she set the sports book back down and headed in my direction.

Just in time, too, because shrieking sounds announced the arrival of the kids. They threw themselves into the cushions and beanbags, then turned themselves in the direction of the empty chair. Zoe grabbed the books out of my hands and thumped down into the seat. "Hey, kids!" she announced. "Let's start with *Sophie's Squash*."

I stood in the back and zoned out as Zoe read. Zoned out enough that Andrea's hand thumping onto my shoulder made me jump again. "Ellie!" she whispered. "I'd like you to do me a favor! That kid in the red shirt is disturbing everyone around him!"

I blinked, focusing on the kids. Sure enough, a little boy all the way on the right was wiggling around in his seat, accidentally kicking the other kids around him. We had only seconds before storytime devolved into chaos.

"Go take him into the stacks and help him pick out a book!" Andrea said. She gave me a gentle push. "Before he melts down!"

I took a step forward. A strange buzzing noise filled my head. "Hey," I whispered at the kid. "Hey, red shirt." All the kids turned around, every single little eyeball focusing on me, waiting for me to speak.

Was the world getting blurry, or was that just me?

Eliana Rachel Katz, age twelve, died
Tuesday afternoon after being swarmed
by a horde of little kids. "Storytime
is boring. Now I have a taste for
blood," one of the children said,
baring sharp little teeth. "Maybe
the children would have spared her
if she'd been more enthusiastic!"
said her supervisor, Andrea Santos!
Currently no funeral is planned, as
the little kids have gone feral and
are busy smacking one another with
the deceased's arm and leg bones.

Sweat popped all along my hairline. I took a shaky
breath, trying to make it deep, except somehow it didn't
all make it into my lungs. So I gasped. I closed my eyes for
a second to get a break from all those eyes.

My eyes sprang open as tiny fingers grabbed my hand.
It was the kid in the red shirt. He was here, looking up at
me trustingly. He was practically a baby. All the other
kids had turned back to watch Zoe read about squash.

My next breath came a little easier. The sweat cooled

on my face. *Breathe.* My dad's voice echoed in my head. And even though he'd been talking to my mom, it felt almost like he was talking to me. *Breathe.* I took a breath in this dark space, then another. *You can do this. He's practically a baby, and who cares what babies think?* So I asked him, "What's your name?"

His foot scuffed the ground. "Ryan. What's yours?"

"I'm Ellie." He wasn't even looking at me anymore. He was looking at the books. Maybe I could do this after all. "Come on. Let's pick something out."

I learned pretty quickly that the only books Ryan cared about were those with trucks on the cover, which made finding him a story easy. Within a few minutes, he was back in his seat with a stack of truck books in his lap, flipping happily through the pages and leaving the other kids alone. He didn't even say thank you or look back at me. Which was perfectly fine, as far as I was concerned.

I might have managed to talk to a stranger, but that was only because he was practically a baby. And I'd barely made it through. Who knew what would happen if I had to do it again?

CHAPTER 9

The b'nai mitzvah DJ is an interesting subspecies of human. They're almost always male, either slightly short or painfully tall, and have something just a little bit off about them: Either they're hairy (and not just a little hairy—like, *really* hairy) or they smell like BO.

Their most distinguishing characteristic? They always think they're much cooler than they really are.

"Yo, whassup, little dude? Home slice!" my bat mitzvah DJ greeted me and Zoe as he walked into our living room. His head, which was topped with a backward trucker hat, nodded at me. "Your hair is on fleek!"

I glowered at him from beneath my definitely not on fleek hair. Because no one said that anymore. No one had said that in years.

My parents didn't sense anything off, however. "Your hat is quite on fleek as well!" said my dad. I just about melted into a puddle and died right there.

But alas, I did not.

The five of us arranged ourselves in the living room: Dad and the DJ on the couch; Zoe and me across from him on the love seat, and Mom seated in the armchair overseeing us all, like its squashy cushions were actually a throne. Hannah, fortunately, was out with one of her many friends doing one of her many activities, so she couldn't sniff her way in. "Can I get you a drink?" Dad asked, doing that weird hovering half stand.

"Sure, man," the DJ said. "I'll have a plastic glass half full of blue Gatorade and half full of orange soda."

Dad deflated a bit. "Sorry, I don't think we have orange soda."

The DJ sighed, pinching the bridge of his nose. "How about Dr Pepper? Coke?"

Dad's eyes brightened as he pushed himself into a full-on stand. "Half blue Gatorade, half Coke coming right up!"

He puttered out into the kitchen. While we waited, the DJ whistled something that sounded like a country song, tapping his fingers in a beat on our table. Zoe watched his fingers. Mom, her eyebrows creased, looked at his face. I stared at the kitchen doorway, waiting for my dad to come back.

It didn't take long before he returned with a glassful of a murky brown substance that looked like a death potion. The DJ took a sip and let out a loud "Ahhhhhh." Dad sat down beside him, looking curiously at the glass. "I'll have to try this concoction of yours once we have orange soda," he said. "It sounds very colorful."

"It is colorful, man," the DJ said. "Both in spirit and in taste."

And in literal color, I thought. But adding that was the least of my worries as the DJ turned to me and Zoe. "Okay, little ladies," he said. "Spill."

By that, I assumed he meant that I should tell him what I wanted for my bat mitzvah. I looked over at Zoe. She nodded at me and pulled out her phone, where we'd jotted down all our notes.

"Ellie asked me to speak for her," Zoe said. "So this is what she wants. Number one." I smiled to myself on the inside, but on the outside I tried to look very serious. "We know that every bat mitzvah is about the kids playing games on the dance floor in between songs, but we decided we don't want that."

The DJ's eyebrows lifted to his hairline, which was pretty impressive, considering how far back his hairline was. "Seriously, no games? What about Coke and Pepsi?" The bat mitzvah classic. "Musical chairs? Limbo? The mummy wrap?"

"I should clarify," Zoe said. "We do want all those games, but not for the kids." She smiled. Her canine teeth looked especially pointy today. I made a mental note to tell her that later. She'd appreciate it, just because of the word *canine*. "We want only the adults playing games."

I didn't see the DJ's reaction, because I was watching my parents. Mom's eyes widened and her brows rose: surprise and confusion. Dad's eyes widened and his lips parted: surprise and a little bit of excitement. The excitement fell away as Mom started speaking, replaced by a firm expression that mirrored hers. "Girls, the adults aren't going to want to play games at your bat mitzvah."

"Yeah, the adults definitely don't want to play games," Dad said a little too quickly.

Zoe's eyes darted to me. "Well, that's what Ellie wants. If the adults don't want to play, then it'll be *your* job"—she looked back at the DJ—"to force them. It'll probably be really unpleasant. You might want to bring a fire hose or something."

"A fire hose?" the DJ repeated. "You sure about that?"

Zoe gave him an elegant shrug. "No. You might also want a Taser."

The DJ's expression was somewhere between horrified and thoughtful. Mom said quickly, "Let's talk about this later, girls. Why don't we talk about music for now?"

Zoe sat up very tall. "Yes, music! We're very excited. We have a *lot* of ideas."

The DJ kept a straight face as Zoe told him all about how much I loved a cappella. "She might actually want you to join in," Zoe said. I confirmed with a nod. "Even if your voice isn't great, we think it adds an authentic aspect to the music."

My parents looked as if they were watching a car careen toward the front of our house, with no sign that it was going to stop.

"Ellie also likes combining sound effects with music in a way you'd never expect. Like ambulance sirens overlaid with Mozart, or the sound of bowling balls falling on the ground mixed with theme songs from children's shows," Zoe said. "Even better if I can bring along my dog and have him howl along to your music." A flicker of something strange—sadness?—shadowed her face for a moment, but then I blinked and it was gone. Weird. "He prefers polka music and songs in extinct languages."

My parents looked as if the careening car had crashed through our front wall and was now continuing straight on toward them.

I gave Zoe a little smile. She nodded back at me. We got this. The DJ would probably run out of here screaming like a car really was heading straight toward him. My parents would be confused, but—

"Zoe," Mom said through clenched teeth. "Would you mind stepping out for a moment? Go have a snack or something."

Zoe and I exchanged a panicked glance. *Oh no. They're onto us.*

But what was she supposed to say back to that? It wasn't like Zoe could ignore my mom and slouch down in her seat to stay. She'd get in big trouble. So with an apologetic frown at me, Zoe hopped up and ran off and left me to the wolves, also known as my parents.

"Ellie," Mom said, looking at me. "You haven't said a word yet. Is this Zoe's idea of a prank?"

"While Zoe's pranks are often humorous, like when she filled our dinner glasses with Jell-O, this really isn't the time for it," Dad said. "This is important, Ells."

He looked serious. My mom looked serious. The DJ looked confused.

But all of them were looking. At me.

The back of my neck prickled. My ears got hot. Everything started to go blurry.

No. *You just did this*, I told myself. *You already talked to someone who was practically a baby, and this grown man is also practically a baby! You can do this!*

I cleared my throat. Opened my mouth. Nothing came out, so I closed it again.

You have *to do this*, I told myself, more firmly this time. *Or else not only will you get stuck with your big bat mitzvah, but Zoe might get in trouble. And that's not okay.*

It was really the idea of Zoe getting in trouble that forced my lips open again. "Yes. I mean, no." My voice came out shrunken and rusty, barely audible. Everybody had to lean in to hear me. I cleared my throat, and this time the words came out a little surer and louder. "I mean, it's not a prank. It's really what I want for my bat mitzvah."

There. I fell back into my seat with a gasp. It had been hard, but I did it. I spoke up. I spoke up, and now everything would be okay. The DJ would cancel, and leave my parents in the lurch, and—

"Your ideas sound awesome, dude!" the DJ exclaimed.

Wait. What?

"I was a little salty when you talked about ambulance sirens, but I *love* the idea of mixing in live dog barks," he said. "You're a real visionary, kid!"

The whole car thing was only a metaphor, but now it felt like that mental car had run me over anyway.

"And games for adults instead of the kids? That's seriously rad, yo. Game-changing. *This* is why I went to DJ school," he enthused.

Dad sat forward, his elbows on his knees, his face lighting up. "Is there actually a school for DJs? Do you know if there's an age limit?"

I slumped even farther back as they talked. I couldn't believe none of this had worked. That I'd managed to speak up in front of this strange adult man, and it still hadn't gotten my bat mitzvah canceled.

You spoke up, a little voice whispered in my head. *You did it. Maybe you* could *do the whole bat mitzvah thing.*

Are you joking? I said back. It probably wasn't a great sign that the voices in my head were talking to each other, but I went on anyway. *This was only one guy. And in English. Totally different than an entire room full of people in Hebrew.* And besides, even if I could physically manage it—which I couldn't—that didn't mean I wanted to. Sure, I had been able to speak, but this whole sweating and shaking thing? Not enjoyable.

Which meant we had way more work to do.

CHAPTER 10

"I know the DJ visit was two days ago, but I still can't get over it," Zoe told me. She handed me a book. I took it, noted the author and title, and slotted it neatly into its proper spot on the library shelf. We made an excellent shelving team. I excelled at alphabetizing, and Zoe excelled at handing me things. "Seriously, he thought dog barks and adults playing games on the dance floor would make for a good bat mitzvah?" She snorted. "I'd like to see my grandparents playing Coke and Pepsi with my grandpa's fake knee. It would probably pop out when he tried to kneel."

"That would be disgusting," I said gloomily. "Which would be on theme for our plan, actually. Considering how disgusting it is that we just made things worse."

Because now if I did end up having this huge bat mitzvah (shudder), it would be to the soundtrack of ambulance sirens and Dogzilla's barking, and none of the kids in my class would get to play any games. "Everything is terrible."

Zoe waited a beat too long before handing me the next book. "I can agree about that."

"Why? What's wrong? Besides the obvious."

She hesitated again. I could practically see the words waiting on the tip of her tongue. "I can't . . . I . . ." She cleared her throat. To my surprise, I realized her eyes were shiny, like she was going to cry. "Not here. I'll tell you later. Distract me for now."

Oh no. Why was Zoe upset? The thought made *me* upset. Had Danny Cohen said something mean to her? I'd beat him up. Well, no I wouldn't, because again: noodle arms. But I could definitely get Hannah to run some sort of smear campaign among her popular friends. By next week, everybody would *know* that Danny Cohen's favorite hobby was picking his nose and eating it, then writing mini reviews of each booger in his notebook like he was a food critic.

"You sure?" I asked her.

She nodded hard, more like she was headbanging at a heavy metal concert than saying yes. And I was a good friend. So I distracted her. "We've tried sabotaging the invitations, the venue, and the DJ, and all three times we made things worse," I said. "But our unlucky streak can't last forever, right? There's still the caterer."

My family and I didn't keep strictly kosher. Sure, we didn't eat things like pork or shrimp, which were forbidden, or mix dairy and meat, also forbidden. But when we were out, we didn't worry so much about what we ate. Like, I've been to restaurants and had salads I'm pretty sure had bacon bits in them, but no big deal, I just picked them out.

I'd tried a bite of a cheeseburger once, and it was good, I guess, but I didn't understand what all the fuss was. And yes, I've tried bacon, too, and same. Whether all the dietary rules still made sense in the modern age or not, I liked being (mostly) kosher and eating the same foods as my ancestors did.

Well, not exactly the same foods as my ancestors did. I was pretty sure my Jewish peasant great-great-great-grandparents scraping a living from the ground in long-ago Poland and Russia hadn't eaten asparagus risotto or sushi or dim sum. I was also pretty sure that they would much rather have eaten those things instead of gruel or raw potatoes or whatever they ate back then.

But anyway.

A lot of the families that would be coming to my bat mitzvah were stricter about their kosher diets than mine—every single thing they ate, in or outside the house, had to be in accordance with Jewish dietary custom. Everything had to be kosher. And because we didn't live in an area like New York City, where there were a lot of Jews, there was only one reputable kosher caterer in town.

If something happened where that kosher caterer could no longer be used, that would be a catastrophe. Because we wouldn't be able to have any food at my bat mitzvah, and how could you have an hours-long party without any food?

"I don't think I can just go ahead and cancel it like I did with the venue," I said. "Mom and Dad already called them about adding more people, and they would've warned the caterer on that phone call to be careful about fake cancellations. No, there's got to be another way."

I thought for a second. "What if their kitchen burned down?"

"Are you serious?" Zoe squealed, which was a good change from her sadness. I smiled a little. I'd been looking for a reaction like that, the ultimate distraction. "You'd get arrested for arson! And maybe hurt people!"

"Okay, so I guess we shouldn't burn anything down." I hung my head as if in disappointment and was rewarded with a tiny giggle from Zoe. Good. The distraction was already working. "So we'll have to figure something else out. When's the next time we're eating their food?"

Zoe pulled out her phone and scrolled through her calendar. I'd always been impressed that she kept one. I was pretty sure I'd never even opened the app. "We have Carl Meier's bar mitzvah in three weekends," she said. "He's got to be using the same caterer."

There was no way to be positively sure without asking his parents, and I wasn't going to do that. But the odds were in our favor. Heavily in our favor. I'd bet all eighty dollars of my Chanukah money on it, because like I said, Goldblum Catering was the only kosher caterer in town.

"Okay, then," I said, taking a deep breath. "Let's shellfish this thing."

Zoe gave me a determined nod. "Let's shellfish this thing." And then she sniffled.

So the distraction clearly hadn't worked. I set my book down on the library cart and grabbed her hand, tugging her behind a shelf. "Tell me what's going on."

She blinked a few times really quickly. "It's Dogzilla. My parents are taking him to the vet right now. We found a lump on his chest." Her chin quivered.

I wasn't sure exactly what that meant, but from the whole crying thing, I could assume it was bad. I flopped a comforting arm over her shoulders. "What kind of lump?"

She sniffled again. "They don't know what kind of lump it is yet. That's why they're taking him to the vet. But I'm worried it might be . . . cancer or something."

Oh. Cancer. Yeah, that was definitely bad. I reached over and gave her a tight squeeze. "I'm so sorry," I said. "But hopefully it's not actually cancer. You don't know anything yet. So we don't need to worry yet, right?"

Suddenly there were footsteps behind us. I tensed, looking over my shoulder. It was Andrea bulldozing in our direction, a smile on her face that looked like a mission. And her eyes were zeroing in on me. Like we were in a horror movie, I heard the sounds of children shrieking in slow motion. It was almost storytime.

I couldn't let her ask me to read to them.

I clapped Zoe on the shoulder. "We'll talk about it later, okay? I have to go to the . . . bathroom." I took off, nearly sprinting across the library floor until I could lock myself safely in a stall. I hid out there until I was absolutely sure storytime must have already started, with Zoe at the helm.

And then storytime was over, and Zoe had to rush out because her dad was in an illegal parking space, and we never actually got to "talk about it later." When I texted her, she just said they'd done tests on Dogzilla's lump at the vet and they'd know more in a few weeks. So we wouldn't have to think about it until then.

For now, we had shrimp to catch.

CHAPTER 11

Three weekends later, Operation Surreptitious Shellfish was officially in motion.

It had taken us a long time to come up with such a great tongue twister of a mission name. *Surreptitious* was the extra-credit word on one of my vocab tests in literacy class. It meant "kept secret, especially because it would not be approved of," which was basically the entire definition of my foolproof, one-hundred-percent-perfect, no-way-it-can-fail plan.

We did Surreptitious Shellfish because shellfish isn't kosher, and Surreptitious Bacon just didn't have the same ring to it.

The plan was simple: Shellfish was not kosher, and the caterer was. So if shrimp somehow turned up in their dishes, there would be a big scandal. My parents would have no choice but to cancel.

And so would everybody else, a small, guilty part of me whispered. *Their business would be totally ruined. And people who made sure to only eat kosher might eat tainted food.*

I shook my head at the voice. *They wouldn't be ruined*, I argued back. *They'll be fine after a little while. And I'll make sure the shrimp is really obvious so nobody who keeps kosher eats it.*

I needed this plan. It involved being quiet and invisible, which were my strengths—maybe my only strengths. What else was I supposed to do? Start a food fight? No, this was the only way. Sorry, Goldblum Catering.

Still, I took an extra-deep breath, trying to clear the guilt out of me.

It didn't work.

I got dressed in one of Hannah's old dresses, a long, sleek, navy-blue faux-silk thing with spirals of glitter over the front. Some of the glitter had come off in the wash, which she warned me about, but I didn't care. It was soft and swishy as it swung against my legs.

I swished around as I texted Zoe some shrimp emojis, then a few question marks. Obviously we had no shrimp in our house, but, fortunately for us, her dad loved shrimp scampi. It was her job to sneak some of those curled-up little shrimpies from their fridge and pack them away in her clutch to bring to Carl's bar mitzvah. Also fortunately (for me), Zoe had been in Carl's class at school last year. I had no idea what I'd do if she hadn't been going with me.

She texted me back with a thumbs-up. Good. Everything was going according to plan.

Then why did I feel so queasy?

In the hallway, Hannah looked me over with a critical eye. "Are you sure you want to wear that? Some of the glitter—"

"Came off in the wash, I know," I said. "But I love it."

She smiled. "Good."

I turned to head downstairs, but she stopped me with a hand on my shoulder. "Want to come in for a second?" she asked. "I can do your makeup."

I was only allowed to wear makeup on special occasions, like b'nai mitzvah, and I'd already been dreading doing it myself, since when I used eyeliner and eye shadow, it tended to make me look like someone had just punched me in the eyes. So it was with only a little hesitation that I followed Hannah through her door, closing it behind me.

Her room wasn't that different from mine in its bones: It had a twin bed with a cheery bright bedspread (yellow for her, pink for me), a desk, a closet, and a window looking out at the opposite side of our house (though there was really nothing interesting to look at on either side).

It was in the details that we differed. In my room, I had the photo board she'd made me on the wall, along with a few pictures of me and Zoe and my parents, and my mom had hung up a couple of paintings she'd found at the thrift store we both liked. Otherwise, my walls were pretty bare. My desk was mostly neat, and I made my bed every day, because it made me feel better to have everything put together.

Hannah's room, on the other hand, was an explosion. Of color: Her walls were covered with pictures of her and her million friends, plus other scraps from her life, like programs from all the plays and musicals she'd appeared in and invitations to all her friends' past b'nai mitzvah. I recognized some faces and names, but there was no way I could keep track of all of them. Of sound: She always had music playing—from where, I wasn't entirely sure. Of *things*: There was just always *stuff* everywhere, from pillows tossed all over her unmade bed to papers and half-finished books overflowing her desk to clothes covering the floor.

"Take a seat," she said. I looked around. The least offensive place to sit was probably her desk chair, so I moved a pile of wrinkled shirts from the chair to the bed.

She came over to my side with her makeup kit. "Close your eyes."

I closed my eyes. I liked it better this way sometimes. There was so much less to focus on.

"So," Hannah said. There was a gentle tugging on my eyelid as she started with eyeliner, and I had to fight the urge not to blink. "What's new in your life lately?"

I wanted to shrug, but I knew it might mess up her steady hand. "Nothing."

"Nothing? At all?" She switched to the other eye. "How about at school?"

"It's summer."

"Right, of course." She was silent for a moment as the tugging returned to the first eye. Hopefully she hadn't messed up. But you know, so what if she had? Makeup was easy enough to wipe off and start again.

Unlike life in general. Sometimes I thought that was

the main reason I had such a hard time interacting with people. Because if you accidentally said something that made you look stupid or mean or whatever, you couldn't just go back and wipe it away. Same if you blurted something out that hurt someone else. Sure, you could say sorry, but that didn't make the hurt disappear or change their first impression of you. The only way to completely avoid the embarrassment or the hurt is not to say anything in the first place.

"How about this summer?" Hannah was truly relentless. It was like her words were a battering ram, and she was hammering away, away, away at the defenses that kept me quiet until I broke open and spilled all my guts to her. But she could hammer away all she wanted: It wasn't going to happen. "What have you and Zoe been up to? How's the library going?"

"Nothing, really," I said. I couldn't exactly tell her what we'd actually been up to! "It's okay."

"Open your eyes," she directed. I opened them to find her like three inches away from my face, staring directly at my eyes. Her minty toothpaste was strong on her breath. I squirmed in my seat. "Okay, the eyeliner looks even to me. Does it look okay to you?"

"Sure," I said.

"You didn't even look."

I took a peek in the mirror. "It looks fine."

She sighed. Why was she sighing? I was telling her what she wanted to hear, wasn't I? "Okay," she said. "Now close your eyes again. I'm going to do some white and silver eye shadow. I think it'll really make your eyes pop with that blue dress. Sound okay?"

"Okay."

This time, she didn't sigh. I closed my eyes, and she got back to work. "You know," she said, and from the way she hesitated before she said it, I knew I wasn't going to like what came next. I tensed up in preparation. "You should really go to some more Kadima events. My friend Eric's little sister is in it, and she's really cool. I bet you'd like her."

I was glad my eyes were closed so that I couldn't roll them. Hannah knew perfectly well why I didn't go to many Kadima events. Because Zoe wasn't Jewish, and you could only join the Jewish youth group if you were Jewish, obviously. "Zoe can't join Kadima."

"I was thinking you could go without Zoe," Hannah said.

Why was she being so mean about my best friend? "I thought you liked Zoe."

"I love Zoe!" Hannah said. "Zoe's great. But it wouldn't hurt to have another friend or two. You *should* be able to do things without each other." The feeling of the eye shadow brush tickling my skin made me shiver. "Come on, there's a social coming up. With food and everything. There will be tons of kids there! Let me introduce you to Sophie."

"Who's Sophie?"

This time, Hannah's sigh gusted me with full-on mint-dragon breath. "Eric's little sister. I *just* told you that."

I was being difficult. I knew who Sophie was. We'd met at one of the first few Kadima events my parents had forced me to go to. "All she did was babble away nonstop about how cute some kid at the next table was," I said. "I didn't even get to introduce myself or anything." Which had, in all honesty, been totally fine with me.

"She was probably nervous," Hannah said. "Just like you. She doesn't have a lot of friends, either. Why not give her a shot?"

Um, for about a thousand reasons. What if we turned

out to hate each other and she turned that hate-energy into mocking me in front of everyone else, making it clear that I'd never have another friend again? What if Zoe and I hung out with her and it turned out Zoe liked Sophie more than she liked me and then Zoe and Sophie ran off to be best friends together, because their names even rhymed? And I never found another best friend because I didn't know anyone whose name rhymed with Ellie, except maybe Smelly Kelly, and I didn't want to be friends with anyone nicknamed Smelly? Because Zoe was the only person who understood that I couldn't do a lot of things like normal people, because of my problem, and maybe Sophie would find out and try to "fix" me and just make me worse?

But I couldn't tell Hannah all of that, so I just gave her a shrug, one small enough that it didn't mess up all her artful eye shadow sweeping.

"You know," Hannah said, "I was just like you once."

I cautiously cracked one eye to see her face. I was sure she'd be laughing, sure that she was making fun of me. But she wasn't. Her expression was dead serious. She'd even lowered the eye shadow brush. Could it be that Hannah might *actually* understand? That she might know exactly what I was going through? "You were?"

"I was," Hannah confirmed. "I know you get nervous talking to new people or in front of crowds. Remember my bat mitzvah?"

Like I could ever forget almost dying.

"You totally freaked out," Hannah continued. "Remember?"

"Hnnnrgh," I said.

She continued on like I hadn't just made a noise like a drowning wildebeest. "When I was your age, I had a hard time talking to new people, too, and I *hated* talking in front of crowds. Once when I had to get up in front of my fifth-grade class to give my final presentation, I just totally froze up. Couldn't remember a word of my speech, no matter how long I'd rehearsed it!"

She shook her head. "I had to ask the teacher to let me use my notes. I almost died of embarrassment, but I used that feeling to get better. I started forcing myself to talk to new people, and you know what?" She didn't wait for me to answer. "The more I did it, the easier it got!"

A bitter taste rose in the back of my throat. Disappointment. Of course Hannah had no idea what I was going through. I *wished* all I had to worry about was freezing up or getting nervous. I closed my eye again.

"Ellie!" My mom's voice echoed down the hallway. "Five minutes!"

I tapped my fingers on my knee. "Are you almost done with my makeup?"

Hannah was silent for a moment. Just when I thought she might not answer, she did. "Yeah. Two more seconds." She rubbed a smidge of eye shadow off the side of my face, then made me do duck lips as she dotted on some light pink lip gloss. "There. Perfect."

I hopped up. "Thanks for the makeup," I said. I focused on quickly leaving her room and hurried back down the hall to grab my bag before Mom really started hollering.

I got all the way into the car before I realized I'd never heard Hannah say, "You're welcome."

CHAPTER 12

My mind whirred with thoughts all through the ride to Carl Meier's bar mitzvah. He was one of the kids in my Hebrew school class I didn't know that well—he sat in the back of the class with Todd Germaine and Danny Cohen, whispering through the teacher's lectures and making up rhyme-alikes for Adon Olam—but it was a policy for my Hebrew school that all the kids in the class got invited to everyone's b'nai mitzvah, so here I was.

I sighed and tilted my head back so that it rested up against the seat. In the mirror overhead, I noticed my mom looking at me quizzically, like she wanted to ask me how I was doing. If I was doing okay.

I closed my eyes so that I didn't have to see it.

I got dropped off at temple comfortably late. B'nai

mitzvah officially began with the start of the morning service, but that was at, like, nine in the morning, and the bar or bat mitzvah kid didn't actually do anything until later. I was used to arriving at ten or ten thirty, when things really got going. So were the rest of the kids in my Hebrew school class.

Not the non-Jewish kids, though. I slid into the back pew next to Zoe, who looked at me with a sour expression. It was similar to the expressions of all the other non-Jewish kids from our regular school class, who'd been sitting here for over an hour as the rabbi and cantor droned on in a language they didn't understand. All their eyes were pretty much dead at this point. "You're late."

"No, you're way early." I shifted on the uncomfortable wooden pew. "Do you have the shrimp?"

I felt that queasy sensation in my stomach again, like I really had to go to the bathroom, except that I'd literally just gone right before walking in here. It was accompanied by a heaviness, like my stomach might actually fall out of my body. Which would be bad.

It felt a little bit like . . . guilt.

"You can't smell them?" Zoe whispered back.

I took a deep inhale and smelled nothing but old

books and musty cushions and a wisp of too-strong floral perfume from one of the old ladies around us. The normal smells of Shabbat service. "Nope."

"Well, that's good," Zoe said. "I wrapped them in, like, a thousand plastic bags." She frowned. "Hopefully that'll be enough to keep me from turning the temple unkosher and going to hell."

"Jews don't believe in hell," I reassured her, but my queasy stomach said otherwise. "And there are lots of things we aren't supposed to be doing in temple. Like, I'm not supposed to be carrying bags in here on Shabbat, but I did anyway."

There were a lot of rules about what Jews are and are not allowed to do on Shabbat, which was our day of rest. The ancient sages and/or actual God had taken the definition of rest super literally, so we weren't allowed to do things like turn things on and off, press buttons like in elevators, or carry things like bags.

We *kind* of kept Shabbat at home, but not that closely. Dad said that if God meant for him to rest, climbing a bunch of stairs instead of pushing one elevator button didn't seem all that restful to him.

"I don't know," Zoe said doubtfully.

I didn't know, either. Because the more I thought about it, the more I worried about it. I'd seen people called out in the media because they'd done something bad. They lost everything, and maybe that would be warranted if you really had done something bad . . . but not if you were being framed, like I'd be doing to Mrs. Goldblum. Could I really do that to Mrs. Goldblum—who had always been perfectly nice to me—and her business? The woman sometimes brought candy to services, for heaven's sakes. And what if somebody who kept seriously kosher *did* accidentally eat some shrimp, or eat off a plate that had touched the shrimp? Maybe they wouldn't die—unless they happened to be allergic to shellfish—but I don't know, making people eat something they didn't want to seemed . . . well, really mean. I didn't like watermelon, because it was basically Styrofoam soaked in sugar water. I always got annoyed with the people who were like, "HeEeEeEre, eat THIS watermelon, it's soooo good," because they couldn't just respect that I didn't want to eat it. And that was just a mild dislike, not a whole dietary preference based on years and years of tradition and religious laws.

It could all be a disaster. And you know what else was

a disaster? I was so deep in my own head that I missed the cue to throw candy at the bar mitzvah boy right after he finished the haftorah blessings, which was the best part of any bar mitzvah. Zoe pegged Carl Meier right in the head, a bull's-eye, while I came in late enough that he was already hiding behind the podium, which didn't get me any points at all.

"Are you totally sure about this?" Zoe asked me when we were standing for the Aleinu. The Shabbat service had a lot of sitting and standing, standing and sitting, and sometimes even going up and down on your toes or bending your knees, which kept you from getting stiff in the uncomfortable seat but also from zoning out or falling asleep.

I took a deep breath. I didn't answer. Not until we stepped outside, squinting in the bright sunlight. "Zoe."

"What?"

"Give me your shrimp."

She gave me that doubtful look again, then looked around before opening her bag, like the kosher police were lurking and ready to arrest her. But nobody even noticed as she pulled out a bag of shrimp and handed it over. I could just make out about five of them through the many Ziploc bags Zoe had used, gray and shiny, mushy and gross. I grimaced as my fingers squished into them.

But I didn't have to hold them long. Just until I threw them in the garbage can.

CHAPTER 13

After services, we had a good six hours before the party started that night. Dad came to pick me and Zoe up, which was great, because he was much more easily persuaded than Mom was. I hopped into the front seat. "You know what would hit the spot?" I said. Not asked, because I wasn't about to give him time to come up with an answer. *"Ice cream."*

A gust of hot air blew in through Zoe's open door, which seemed to second our point. "Ice cream would be amazing right now," she said.

It truly would. Because I had some serious scheming to do in the next six hours, and some sugar would make it go down a lot easier.

"I'm supposed to take you two home for lunch," Dad

said, but he sounded thoughtful. He was already halfway there. I just had to bring him to the finish line.

"Ice cream can be lunch," I said.

That was all he needed. Soon enough we were pulling into Dairy Queen, where the air-conditioning blasted us in the face as we walked inside. "You girls should get some real food, too," Dad said, and then he went and ordered a large chocolate Blizzard like a giant hypocrite.

"What happened to real food?"

"I guess ice cream is real food," Dad said, which was great, because it meant Zoe and I could get large Blizzards for lunch, too.

We sat outside, because ice cream tastes best in the hot summer air. (The heat makes it all drippy and extra sweet. It's scientifically proven. At least to my mouth.) I took a few bites, then a few more bites, then a few *more* bites because it was melting, and then turned my attention to our scheming. I opened my mouth, looking at Zoe, and—

"I think they gave me extra chocolate," Dad said happily.

Right. Dad was there. Zoe and I exchanged a worried glance. She was going to come back to my house before the party that night, so we could also plan then. But time was running out. "Hey, Dad," I said. "Can you get us some extra napkins?"

He scrunched his forehead in confusion. "We have a lot of napkins right here." He patted the stack of napkins on the table.

"Right, I know," I said, but he was still looking at me oddly. So I tapped my head. "Um, brain freeze."

Dad nodded like that made total sense.

Zoe coughed. "I have to go to the bathroom," she said. "Ellie, want to come?"

Good thinking, Zoe! "I was just thinking that I had to go to the bathroom!" I cried. "Let's go!"

Dad's forehead scrunched even farther this time. "Isn't the bathroom in there just a single stall?"

Zoe and I shifted uncomfortably in our seats. That killed *that* plan. "Weird, I don't have to go anymore," I said.

"Me neither," said Zoe.

Dad's forehead scrunched so much I got a flash-forward of what he'd look like in fifty years.

Okay. If we couldn't get Dad to leave us alone, and we couldn't go somewhere alone, that left only one option. "Hey, Zoe," I said. "You know our . . . gift for Carl? About how we decided to change what we were . . . giving him?"

Zoe took a giant bite of ice cream, then nodded as she swallowed. "Do you have any new ideas?"

"Does your mother know about this?" Dad asked. "Didn't she give you a card and a check?"

"Not that gift," I said. A hot wind dusted our table with sand and a few crumpled napkins. Somewhere distant behind us, I could hear the garbled chatter from the drive-through window. "Um, Zoe and I were getting him a . . . *special* gift. In addition to the check. Because we're such good friends and all."

"I've literally never heard you mention this kid," Dad said.

Shoot. "Right, we're not actually *that* good of friends," I said hastily, and exchanged a look with Zoe. "It's just that . . . Zoe has a big crush on him."

A glob of ice cream fell from Zoe's mouth and splatted on the table.

"I see," Dad said, and did what I thought was supposed to be a wink, except it was actually more of a hard blink. "Well, don't let me interrupt you girls, then!"

Zoe gave me a dirty look. No, that was definitely more than a dirty look. More of a death glare. "I think it's too late to get another physical thing for him," she bit off. "I think our only option is really to . . . do some kind of performance."

"A performance?" I echoed. I had no idea what she meant. "Like . . . what?"

Zoe frowned. "Like, making a commotion. Something big and loud. To make everyone . . ." She cleared her throat. "Um, extra happy!"

By which she meant *un*happy. So she thought we should make a big fuss in order to outrage everybody at the party. Including Mrs. Goldblum and the caterers. "I don't know," I said slowly. "I'd much rather bring some kind of . . . gift."

Zoe stared at me. I stared at Zoe.

"Girls, I'm on Zoe's side," my dad said helpfully. "She's the one with the crush, after all."

"Yeah, Ellie," Zoe growled. "*I'm* the one with the crush."

Zoe glared at me. I glared at Zoe.

"I feel like I'm missing something," said Dad.

The sound of a phone chiming interrupted our

standoff. Zoe's phone. She broke off our mutual glare to pull it out of her pocket. "Oh," she said. "My mom's asking where we are." Her fingers started flying. "I'll just let her know we're—" She stopped as it chimed again. "Huh. She says I should come home right away." She looked up. "It's like she has weird mom radar to know that I'm eating ice cream for lunch."

I scraped the bottom of my cup with my spoon. "I'm done anyway."

The ride to Zoe's house was quiet. We were both disappointed that our hangout time got cut short. I hugged her goodbye, knowing I'd be seeing her soon.

And that I wouldn't be any closer to a plan when I did.

CHAPTER 14

By the time we showed up at the country club that night, I was kind of regretting throwing out all our shrimp. "I really don't want to make some kind of commotion," I told Zoe as we walked inside, tottering on our high-heeled shoes. "Did you have any more ideas?"

She didn't answer me. She stayed quiet, her eyes focused on the ground before her. What was up with her?

"So I was thinking," I continued. Maybe she just needed a prompt. "Anything we would do to get my parents to cancel the catering wouldn't reflect well on them. We'd have to poison the food or something."

That should get her, the same way she'd jumped on me about the whole arson thing. I stopped and waited for her to answer with an, *Oh my God, Ellie, I am not going to jail for attempted murder.* I already had my response stored up. *It's not murder if you just make people sick, right?*

Let's get one thing straight: I had zero intentions of poisoning anyone or making anybody sick. I just wanted Zoe to respond.

But she just kept staring at the ground. I snuck a glance, too. There was nothing down there but sidewalk speckled with flattened circles of gum. What was *up* with her?

"And obviously we're not going to poison the food," I said. If she was actually listening, she'd comment about how suspiciously disappointed I sounded, but really that was because she wasn't listening to me at all. "And if we can't get my parents to cancel the catering, then, well, we have to make them cancel on us. Like we tried to do with the DJ, except this time we're going to be so bad that it actually works." As much as I didn't want it to be true, Zoe had been kind of right: If she hadn't come up with any miraculous solutions in the few hours we'd been apart, we would have to make some kind of commotion. I'd had an idea at home. One I really didn't want to go through with.

But it seemed like our only option.

I quieted down as we passed inside. The woman greeting people at the door stared at me a second too long as I walked inside with Zoe. I wondered if she was Ms. Winters. If she was thinking, *Aren't you supposed to be dead?*

Once safely inside the lobby, I went on. "I already did the first part of the plan. I went on Mom's laptop and created a fake email address, then emailed Goldblum Catering to ask them about a huge event on my bat mitzvah day."

That drew a reaction from Zoe. "What? Why?"

I smiled. "Because they won't worry that they'll be losing business by canceling on us. All we have to do is convince them that this hypothetical event would be way better than mine."

"And how are you going to do that?" That was a bit more like the old Zoe. Even if her voice was still a little dull.

"How are *we* going to do that, you mean." Because there was no way I could do this all by myself. Or that I could do it at all. I was really going to need to depend on Zoe for this. Like, a lot. So it kind of annoyed me that she was seeming so off right now. I needed to be able to depend on my best friend.

"Whatever." Zoe stopped by the bathroom door. "I have to pee."

I had to pee, too. I always had to. So we went in, did our business, and then stood at the sink washing our hands. I gazed at the two of us in the mirror. Both of our eyebrows were pulled together, like we were in a competition to see who could get a unibrow first. I was nervous, but seriously, what was up with Zoe? "Zoe, what's—"

The bathroom door creaked open behind us. I stopped speaking mid-sentence and lowered my gaze to the sink, like I was making sure my hands were scrubbed perfectly clean.

"Oh, Ellie and Zoe. Hey." It was Sophie, the girl Hannah had told me to befriend. She smiled at us, showing a mouth full of silver braces.

"Hey, Sophie," Zoe said. "What's up?"

"Just peeing."

"Yeah, us too."

Oh my God, we did not have time for any conversation right now, much less a conversation about bodily functions. "Hi," I said, giving Sophie a close-lipped smile, because if all I said was hi, there was no way to embarrass myself and start my stomach a-churning.

Though what about tone? What if my voice squeaked or sounded too eager? My stomach started to churn.

I had to pee again.

"We'd better go," I said, my hands locking around Zoe's elbow. I pulled her out of the bathroom into the hallway, where women in dresses and pantsuits were already forming a line. I ducked around the corner, where there was no line for the men's room. There was never a line for the men's room, which didn't seem fair.

As soon as we stopped, Zoe scowled at me. "Why'd you do that?"

I looked at her blankly. "Do what?"

"Literally drag me away from Sophie Herrmann."

"I did not literally *drag* you away from Sophie Herrmann." Okay, maybe I did literally drag her away from Sophie Herrmann. But why was my stomach still churning? I could say *anything* to Zoe without her judging me or getting annoyed with me. That was the purpose of a best friend. "We have something important to do, and I wanted to make sure we got it done."

"But we could've taken a minute and been nice to Sophie," Zoe said. "I like Sophie."

Oh no. That was why my stomach was churning. I'd predicted this. Zoe liking Sophie more than me and running off to be best friends with Sophie instead of me. It was really happening, and without me even becoming friends with Sophie in the first place. How could Zoe do this to me? Not just befriend Sophie, but get mad at me? Like I'd done something wrong?

I pushed it out of my mind, but that only pushed it down into my throat, where it got stuck. A man walked by, looking down at me curiously. Beads of sweat rose all over my forehead, prickling. My feet were suddenly wet. I had no idea how to respond. How to deal with this. How could I make the caterers cancel on me alone? I needed Zoe to do this. I needed Zoe—

Again, my dad's voice echoed inside my head like Mufasa from *The Lion King* speaking to Simba from the sky. Like he was talking to me in the future and not my mom in the past. *Breathe, Liz. Just stop for a moment and take a few deep breaths.*

I couldn't afford to die now, so I did it. I held my breath for a moment, even though my body kept trying to heave in air. Then I sucked in a deep breath. The air flooded my body, which could have fanned the flames, but it didn't. It blew some of them out. Made the fire smaller. Less consuming.

So I did it again. And again. And even though my stomach tried to start churning again, tried to scream at me, *You're taking too long, she's going to walk away, look at her judging you, she thinks you're an idiot, she hates you*, I waited till I'd breathed out to speak again.

With another person I didn't know as well, that whole Mufasa mantra wouldn't have worked. I would've been absolutely convinced it was true and whoever it was now hated me. But this was Zoe. I knew every twitch of her face as well as I knew my own, and yeah, she was irritated right now, but she didn't hate me.

"We can hang out with Sophie later," I said. Sophie was one variable too many to deal with at this moment. "We have a lot to do right now."

Zoe just scowled harder, carving lines deeper into her face. But I grabbed her hand and squeezed, and the lines relaxed. She sighed. "What do you need me to do?"

"I have to make sure that the absolute last thing they want to do is cater my bat mitzvah." Which, come to think of it, meant that Zoe couldn't be the only one misbehaving. It would *have* to be me. And they'd have to know it was me, too.

My armpits got sweaty again at the very thought. There was no way I could do this. We'd done a unit on ancient Greek mythology in social studies earlier this year and learned about Icarus, who'd built himself wax wings so that he could fly. And he did, swooping all through the sky in triumph. But then he pushed it and flew up near the sun, which melted his wax wings and sent him plummeting down through the sky and into the water, which—I looked this up—would have killed him instantly, because smashing into the water from a great height is really no different from smashing into concrete.

Now I was Icarus. I'd pushed this too far, and I was flying near the sun, and if I went any closer, I would die.

Eliana Rachel Katz, age twelve, died
of dehydration at Carl Meier's bar
mitzvah after sweating out her entire
body's worth of water. "Very strange.
It's almost like she was on the surface
of the sun," said the medical examiner.

Zoe Sharp added, "I'm very sad, and
so is my best friend, Sophie Herrmann."
The bar mitzvah boy and his guests
did not notice anyone was missing and
feasted upon their kosher meal with
aplomb.

I took another deep breath, making sure to exhale it
all the way out before I took another. It was helping, so
why not keep going? It helped enough, at least, to tell
her exactly what we had to do. "We have to start a food
fight," I said, taking yet another deep breath. "And not
just any food fight. The food fight to end all food
fights."

She wrinkled her forehead at me as we entered the
main hall. Waiters and waitresses in crisp white coats
were already circulating throughout the room with silver
trays held up on one hand. Some stopped at groups of
people to offer them mini chicken tacos or hamburger
sliders, while others refreshed the veggie table. Zoe and I
liked to station ourselves wherever the waiters and waitresses came from, because then we got first dibs on all the
snacks, whereas all the people at the far end of the room

got stuck with trays full of used toothpicks and crumpled napkins.

We pushed our way through the crowd, ducking below plates and glasses of wine, making a pit stop at the veggie table to cram some nuts and crackers into our mouths. Then we grabbed some mini hot dogs and sliders off the circulating trays, which led us to a position safely against the wall on the far side of the room, where we could see everything going on. "I don't know," Zoe said. "Wouldn't that kind of ruin Carl's bar mitzvah?"

"Look how bored he looks," I said. It was true. Carl was alone in the corner, shoving food into his face, his expression unhappy. "This isn't exactly his scene. But he would love a food fight! Remember the one he started last year at lunch?" It had been epic. Mrs. Miller had taken a plate of meat loaf to the face. "Even if he'd hate it, it's either ruin Carl's bar mitzvah, the Goldblums' catering business, or my entire life. There's not really a contest there."

Zoe just raised an eyebrow.

"Seriously," I continued. "Carl's family might be upset about a food fight, but are you really trying to tell me Carl wouldn't be absolutely delighted to have a massive food fight erupt at his bar mitzvah?" I snuck another glance over at Carl. Tall, red-haired, and gawky, he was stuffing about as many sliders down his gullet as he could without choking to death. Note that I didn't just say choking, because he was doing a little of that, pausing every so often to cough up a soggy bit of bread or meat. "It's really a present to him, if you think about it. He'll get to throw food at his friends and his family and not even get blamed for it."

I expected Zoe to put up more of a protest, but she only cocked her head thoughtfully. "You know, you're probably right about that."

I had been exactly right. Because Carl wouldn't get blamed for it: *I* would.

My stomach flipped over at the very thought.

CHAPTER 15

Food fights are easy enough to start. I'd seen enough of them in the cafeteria to know that. All you have to do is stand up, yell, and throw something from your plate at someone else. Preferably the food is something that travels well through the air, like a bread roll or gloppy ball of mashed potatoes, rather than chili or green beans, and you actually hit the person somewhere like the forehead, which would make them mad enough to throw something, too.

But this wasn't just any food fight. This had to be the food fight to *end* all food fights. Operation Surreptitious Shellfish was no longer surreptitious. It had to be Operation Blatant Shellfish (another vocab word). Even if there was no more shellfish involved. Actually, could

I bring bacon back into this? Operation Blatant Bacon had a much better ring to it.

I was just stalling. The cocktail hour was ending, and we were getting herded toward the main dining room. Usually they did the candle-lighting ceremony, a welcome speech, and then everybody got to eat dinner, even though I bet the number of people who were actually hungry after downing trays full of bruschetta toasts and mini tacos was approximately zero. Which meant I had to plan. Quickly.

As soon as Zoe and I found our spots at the kids' table, I swiveled around, taking note of everything in the room. If this bar mitzvah was anything like every single other bar mitzvah I'd attended over the past couple of years, then we kids would be getting chicken fingers and French fries, a perfectly respectable entrée. In a normal food fight, I could toss my chicken fingers and fries, then Zoe's chicken fingers and fries, and get a good rumble started.

But again, this wasn't just any food fight. It had to be bigger. Messier. Gloppier.

And for that, I needed the adult entrées. Steaks. Chicken breasts. Vegetarian pasta dishes. All with lots of sauce.

There! I ignored Carl as he began unhappily mumbling his way through his candle-lighting ceremony and zeroed in on the carts rolling through the swinging kitchen doors. Because kosher food had all sorts of rules and you couldn't mix meat and dairy—not even cooked in the same pan at different times—it couldn't be cooked in just any kitchen. My temple had two separate kitchens, one for meat and one for dairy products like milk, butter, or cheese. Since the kitchen at the country club wasn't kosher, Mrs. Goldblum and her staff would have prepared the food somewhere else and brought it all here to be warmed up.

The carts stopped along the wall, waiting for Carl to finish with the candle-lighting ceremony. I nudged Zoe with my elbow. It was now or never. "Ready?" I hissed. It would be fine. She'd be by my side the whole time. I'd just follow her—

She shook her head, her eyes fixed across the table. I went to see what she was looking at. Danny Cohen. Of course. Danny Cohen was sitting across from us, and he was looking at Zoe and smiling.

I nudged her again. "It has to be now," I whispered. "If we let them serve the food, it'll be too late." I guess we could have waited for the cake, but I did not have a very good relationship with bar mitzvah cake.

She shook her head again, stubbornly this time, her fancy dangly earrings swinging on the sides of her head. "You didn't even ask me what was wrong, Ellie," she said, and I realized, to my horror, that her dark eyes were really, really shiny. "We got Dogzilla's test results back."

"And he's going to be totally fine?" I whispered hopefully, but my heart plummeted even as I said it. Maybe this wasn't about Danny Cohen after all.

And yet, as she started talking about what it meant for a dog to have cancer and that maybe it didn't mean he was going to die soon but she was still worried, my eyes strayed back to the carts. Carl was on his grandparents. The number of unlit candles on the cake was dwindling, my time to act along with them. My heart started to pound faster. If I didn't go through with the food fight right now, then everything would be ruined.

"I'm really sorry," I whispered. Zoe stiffened. "Please, can we talk about it later, though? We have to do this *now*."

She lowered her chin to the table. I sat there for a moment, giving her time to change her mind . . . but she wouldn't even look at me.

Fine, let her be mad. I could do this all on my own.

Maybe if I repeated it enough times, I'd actually start to believe it.

"Hey," Danny Cohen was saying as I stood up and started creeping away. "Your dog is sick?" I couldn't hear any more once I got farther away. Everybody was busy clapping for Carl's dads, so nobody noticed me. Perfect. I was almost there. Just five more steps. Four more. Three—

A woman in a white coat stepped right in front of me. "Can I help you?" she said, her eyes drilling into my face.

My breath caught in my throat. I couldn't even take a deep one to try to control the flames. They were rising up, getting ready to roar and probably scorch me from the inside out.

If only Zoe were here. She'd know exactly what to say. Or at least she'd manage to say *something*. Anything. She wouldn't be standing here with her mouth hanging open like a fish caught on a line.

"You should get back to your seat." The woman was still staring down at me, her eyebrows raised impatiently. "Go on. You don't want to get in the way of the servers."

"Uh . . ." I tried to force out some words. What could I say that would make her let me past? I hiccuped. The flames roared inside me, burning any words that might have risen up.

She rolled her eyes and grabbed me by the arm maybe a little harder than she had to, then marched me back to the kids' table. I climbed back into my seat beside Zoe, the flames dulling into some hot coals, settling into embarrassment in my stomach.

Footsteps behind me. "Ms. Winters, we need you in the kitchen!" someone said breathlessly to the woman who'd walked me over. She walked away briskly, leaving me staring after her.

Ms. Winters. That had been the woman I'd so successfully fooled over email. It was bizarre how different it was in person like this. Once again, I wished that real life could be more like email, where I could figure out what I wanted to say first, then look it over to make sure there weren't any stupid errors.

Wait.

Wait.

Maybe I *could* do that. Or at least something like it. If I could do it quickly, because Carl was about to blow out his candles, and then it wouldn't be long before they started serving the main courses. I propped my chin up on my hands, ignoring Zoe's curious look, and closed my eyes.

Against the darkness of my eyelids, I pictured myself back in front of the food carts, blocked by Ms. Winters. Just as in real life, my throat closed up with panic. But this time, because she was only a figment of my imagination, she didn't say anything or yell at me. She just stood there, frowning.

In my head, I tried telling her that I was looking for the bathroom. She didn't frown as much as she had before, but she didn't let me past, because I knew perfectly well that the bathrooms were back toward the entrance.

What could I tell her that wouldn't get me sent away? I thought about saying that I was just curious about what the entrées would be, but I figured that all she'd do was quickly rattle off the menu before shooing me away. I could say that I was looking for my friend, but that didn't make any sense, because the only people who were there around the food were the white-coated employees of the catering company or the country club, not any kids.

But . . . what if I was looking for someone who *was* supposed to be there? *My mom is one of the caterers, and I need to ask her something*, I imagined saying.

No—I went back and revised. Maybe I should phrase it more like my mom was literally right there, and I just had to get over to her. I could crane my neck a little bit and raise my eyebrows, like I was seeing her.

I took a deep breath. Maybe I could actually do this.

I hopped back up—the adults were all crunching away on their salads and bread rolls, the entrées poised to go—and headed over toward the carts. Thank goodness Ms. Winters had been called away. And you know, going back this second time felt easier, since I'd already taken these steps before.

Five steps left. Four steps. Three—

"Can I help you?" It was a man in a white coat this time. All I had to do was bluff my way past him. His name tag said Judd, but I renamed him Mr. Winters to make him fit better into my rehearsal.

I held my shoulders back. Cleared my throat. Said the words I'd gone over and over in my head. "My mom's just right there." I jutted my chin at a vague area behind him. "I have to ask her something."

Fake Mr. Winters nodded, like what I'd said made total sense. "Go ahead," he said, then glanced down at his waist as his radio began to crackle. As I focused, the crackling static also focused into words. *Come in . . . Judd . . . Spill . . . broken glass . . .*

He said some words I would definitely get in trouble for as he rushed past me and out the door. Good. One down. I held my shoulders back as far as they could go, almost as if they were wings, as I moved forward, right up to the carts.

But first I glanced over my shoulder at Zoe. She wasn't even looking at me. So she hadn't noticed the big step I'd taken. It felt kind of like a bee sting deep inside me.

Whatever. If I'd managed to talk to this strange adult and get where I needed to go, that shimmering feeling of pride would have to be enough. So what if it mostly got buried by the anxiety and the fear about what came next? Somehow I knew that the fire wouldn't be able to burn it away.

Swinging doors opened. Out stepped Mrs. Goldblum, who I recognized from temple. *Good,* I thought, even if I wasn't sure whether I should be thankful or sad that she'd be here to witness what came next. Thankful, because she knew me, and it would make her decision to cancel on me much easier. Sad, because I liked her perfectly well, and sometimes she gave me candy, and what

I was about to do was so bad that I wouldn't deserve candy anymore.

She murmured to one of the other caterers, who I vaguely recognized but didn't know. *Huge event . . . lots of money . . . but . . . Ellie Katz's bat mitzvah . . .*

Their words gave me resolve. All they needed was a little push—or okay, a push to end all pushes—and they'd skip on my bat mitzvah.

I reached for the closest plate.

CHAPTER 16

My heart was pounding in my ears. The flames were leaping, tickling heat in my stomach and my chest. Only two things kept them from totally consuming me. The deep breaths, which I kept taking until my head started feeling light. And the run-through of events in my head, spelling out what exactly I wanted to do and how I would react if a number of things happened to me.

My fingers squished into a saucy white chicken breast, which dripped something green and oily onto the carpet as I lifted it. I had enough time to see Mrs. Goldblum's dark eyes widen in pleasant surprise as she noticed me, then keep widening with horror as she realized what I was about to do. "Ellie Katz, what are you—"

I threw the chicken. No, I *hurled* the chicken. Either

way, it went soaring through the air in a beautiful arc, dripping grease onto people's heads all the way, and landed with a *splat* on the side of Carl Meier's head.

I couldn't look at Mrs. Goldblum. *I'm really sorry*, I thought in her general direction. She was surely looking at me with shock and disbelief, just like everybody else in the room, who all had to be looking in my direction. Their eyes. All on me. I couldn't bring myself to look, but they all had to be staring at me, right? There must have been at least two hundred of them. The weight of their combined gaze threatened to crush my chest in. I gasped in a breath. The flames roared in delight.

No. No, I still had more to do. This wasn't enough.

I focused on Carl Meier's face, half-covered in gloopy green sauce. His eyes were so wide I could see the whites all around the blue irises, his lips stretching as if in slow motion. What if he didn't actually like the food fight? What if I'd just ruined his big day? He was going to scream, he was going to cry, he was going to—

—*grin wider than I'd ever seen.* "FOOD FIGHT!" he bellowed, diving for the closest basket of bread rolls.

As if following a general's war cry, Todd Germaine and Jared Novin quickly leaped into action. "FOOD

FIIIIIIIIGHT!" they shouted in response. Steaks—the caterers must have started serving on the other side of the room—went flying. Other kids joined in the battle cry. Chicken fingers fell from the air like rain.

Victory swelled through me, expanding my rib cage. The fire was still burning, but there was enough room in me to keep it from eating me up. The focus was off me now, after all. I grabbed another chicken breast, a handful of pasta, a big scoop of mashed potatoes, and hurled them all into the now-teeming crowd. It was amazing how quickly a neat, orderly bar mitzvah could turn into chaos.

Chaos smelled pretty good, as it turned out.

I wiped my hands on Hannah's dress. It didn't fit her anymore, so she wouldn't care that it was ruined. A job well done.

Well, almost done.

My heart fell as I realized what part I still had left to do. I turned to find Mrs. Goldblum staring at the chaos. She looked totally lost, seeing all of her hard work go to waste.

And then she turned to me. Narrowed her eyes. "Ellie Katz," she said. "If you think . . ." She trailed off, letting the words hang menacingly in the air. It was worse than spelling out exactly what I should be thinking. I mean, *I* knew what I was thinking and feeling. Kind of like I wanted to shrivel into a ball of mashed potatoes and have somebody throw me across the room and splatter me against the wall. I felt a little bit like I deserved it.

Mrs. Goldblum's words came back in a rush. "If *you think* I'm going to do this all over again in just a few months, you're wrong!"

I held my breath with anticipation. Was she going to . . .

"You're going to have to find another caterer for your bat mitzvah!" she cried.

Yes. I did my best to hide my triumphant smile. She stared hard at me, as if waiting for me to fall at her feet and apologize, but of course I wasn't going to do that. Was she going to yell anything else at me?

No. Nothing. So I turned and disappeared into the churning crowd. Some adults had taken shelter in the hallway that led to the bathrooms, and a few unlucky grandparents in the middle of the room were covered in food, tomato sauce dripping down bald heads and spotting silver buns. *Sorry, sorry, sorry,* I thought at them as I rushed through the kids hollering and painting the room with food—there were a few advantages to being small and almost invisible—to where Zoe had taken refuge with Sophie and a few other girls in the corner, barricaded by extra chairs.

The other girls turned to me, and I thought they might yell at me for starting this whole thing and messing up their dresses, but instead, Sophie said breathlessly, "Isn't this wild? Can you believe Carl started a food fight at his own bar mitzvah?"

Really? She thought Carl Meier had started it? I glanced over at the other girls to find all of them but Zoe nodding in agreement. Zoe was staring intensely past me into the chaos of the room.

"You got really unlucky, Ellie," Sophie continued, still breathlessly. She really ought to stop and take a good deep breath. If I could possibly say more than three words to her without sweating out all my body's liquid, I'd tell her how helpful I'd found them. She nodded at me with sympathy. "Were you going to the bathroom or something? It looks like you got caught right in the middle of it."

My eyebrows shot up my forehead as I realized what she was really saying. *We all have no idea you're the one who started the food fight, Ellie. Even if you think we're all staring at you all the time, we were actually paying zero attention as you took the risk of your life. And if we didn't see it, that means probably no one but Mrs. Goldblum saw it, and maybe there's actually a chance of your parents not finding out what you did.*

My cheeks heated up as I realized Sophie and the others were still staring at me, waiting for a response. "Yeah," I said weakly. "I guess I did get unlucky."

CHAPTER 17

There was only so much food at this bar mitzvah, and so, after what felt like ten hours but was probably more like ten minutes, the projectiles started running out, smashed into the carpet or splattered on people's fancy clothes. I huddled behind the chairs with Zoe, Sophie, and the other girls as Ms. Winters and the other country club workers circled around the room, seeming unsure about what to do. I spotted Carl Meier's dads, who looked furious and were coated in oil. Their eyes focused on their son, but they still didn't seem to want to yell at him. It *was* his bar mitzvah, after all.

Eventually, we got ushered into another ballroom, where the dance floor was hastily cleared for us kids to play games as they cleaned the other room and, I don't know, maybe slapped together some kosher egg salad sandwiches or something. I tagged along with the other girls, grabbed on to Zoe's sleeve, and held her back from going to the table.

"What?" she hissed at me, which I took as an encouraging sign, because it meant that at least she was speaking to me. I pulled her into the corner of the room behind a tangle of plastic-covered tables. When she stopped, she turned to me and crossed her arms. A spaghetti noodle dangled from her hair, but this didn't seem like the best time to tell her. "Did you bring me back here to kill me?"

I rolled my eyes. "Stop being ridiculous."

"I'm not being ridiculous," she said. "Sure, I don't think you're a murderer, but I didn't think you'd ever start a food fight, either."

That was true. I was different, I realized to some surprise. I'd started a food fight. I'd talked to strangers. "We can talk about Dogzilla now," I said. "I'm really sorry I had to leave before."

She glared at me. "Oh, so now that you have some spare time, we can care about me?"

Her words stung. She'd gotten this all wrong. "It's not that I don't care about you. Of course that's not true,"

I said. "It's just more important that we did that food fight." Because it was time sensitive. Dogzilla would still be sick in an hour. "And I really needed you there with me."

Zoe's face went hard and flat. "Seriously? Your stupid plan is *more important* than my dog having *cancer* and maybe *dying*?" That last word came out with a shuddery gasp. It made me want to hug her.

Zoe was still busy glaring at me, though. The shuddery gasp faded away. "I don't want to talk to you right now. I don't want to cry in the middle of Carl's bar mitzvah."

"Zoe, that's not—"

She stepped past me. I started to follow, but she was moving quickly away. Toward where Danny Cohen was standing with his friends. I hesitated a moment, then walked to the table where Sophie and the other girls were sitting. Zoe probably just needed some time alone to cool off.

I hadn't been a bad friend, right? She'd agreed to help me. It wasn't like I'd forced her.

She didn't want to do this in the first place, a tiny voice whispered in my head. *You did kind of make her. And she's going through a lot. She was here for you, but were you really there for her?*

"I kind of want a food fight at my bat mitzvah now," one of Sophie's friends, Eva Karp, was saying. Eva had always seemed nice, even if she had the last name of a fish. She turned to me. "What do you think, Ellie?"

I gave her a noncommittal shrug. "Maybe," I said, then jumped on the inside. I'd talked! In front of the group!

None of them even acknowledged this as a big deal, though. Sophie just said, "I wouldn't want all the food getting on my dress, though."

"I'd wear a poncho," Eva said, and a third girl, Jana Hart, giggled. I giggled a little bit, too, at the thought of Eva wearing a clear plastic rain poncho over her fancy, puffy bat mitzvah dress. What if it wasn't a clear poncho, though? What if it was—

"A fancy poncho," I said, then cringed on the inside. That was a real thing I'd just said. Not a single boring word like *maybe*, but a real thing they could hear and cringe at and think I was stupid for saying! Well, my voice had been super quiet. Maybe they hadn't heard me.

But they did. And they laughed. I shrank back for a

moment, because obviously they were laughing at me. "Yeah," Eva said. "With diamonds and lace on it!"

"I want mine to be Gucci," Jana said, and they all giggled again. And then I giggled with them, a second too late. Because they weren't laughing at me. They were laughing at what I'd said. And honestly, it felt kind of good.

But not as good as it would've felt to talk to Zoe. She avoided me the whole rest of the bar mitzvah, only showing up when it was time for my mom to drive us both home. With us both crammed into the back seat, surely we'd be able to talk.

Only, that was hard when she wouldn't talk to me.

Or look at me.

By the time Mom pulled into Zoe's driveway, I was simmering between my ears. "I'll walk Zoe to the door," I said, unclicking my seat belt.

Mom looked tired. One of her eyes twitched. She hadn't said anything when she saw the state of our dresses. I was sure that interrogation was coming later. "It's late, Ellie. You guys can hang out—"

A shrill ringing came from her purse. She frowned even deeper and rummaged around in her bag, pulling out her phone. "Hello? . . . Yes, this is Liz Katz. . . . Oh, hi, Patricia!"

I froze. Mrs. Goldblum's first name was Patricia.

"How are you— Sorry, what? What was that?" Mom's voice lowered, and she curled into herself, like if she hid her mouth from me, I wouldn't be able to hear her. "A conflict? What are you—" She turned to me suddenly. "Ellie, go walk Zoe to the door. Go ahead." I hesitated, wanting to hear the rest of the conversation, but her eyes narrowed at me. She wouldn't be continuing this conversation as long as I could hear. *"Now."*

I hopped out of the car. Zoe had somehow already made it almost all the way to her front door. I had to run to get in front of her. And stumble back when she plowed into me. But I stood strong. "We need to talk," I said through clenched teeth, echoing my mom.

"Oh, do we?" She stepped to the side. I got ready to jump in front of her again, but she only toed at the dirt to the side of the walk, pushing up little hills in the grass.

"Yeah." I glanced back at my mom's car, but she appeared to be yelling into her phone. I turned again to Zoe. "Look, you understand why I thought my situation was more important than yours at that second, right? I wasn't saying it was more important overall."

Zoe kicked out. Her hills collapsed. "No, Ellie. I don't

understand." Her feet stomped down onto the collapsed hills, returning them to flat ground. "I thought I understood. I thought you were my *friend*."

"It wasn't a matter of friendship," I said hotly. "It was a matter of actual life and death."

Suddenly a realization floated through my head. About how I kept assuming and feeling like I'd die when I did these difficult things . . . and yet, I didn't. The worst almost never came to pass. I assumed I'd die when my parents found out about my invitation sabotage, and when I had to help that little kid, and at Carl Meier's bar mitzvah, and more. But each time, I didn't die.

But that didn't mean I could do a full-on bat mitzvah. No. That was on a whole other level.

Zoe snorted. "Yeah, okay. It's time to get over yourself, Ellie. You're not the only one with problems." As if on cue, Dogzilla started barking from inside the house, his shrill, throaty howl piercing even through the closed door. "Your bat mitzvah isn't life and death. Do you know how selfish you sound when you say that when my dog might *literally* die?" Her voice trembled as she said that last word.

"I'm not selfish," I argued. My heart lurched in my

chest. "And of course I care about Dogzilla. He's why I'm donating to the animal rescue!"

"You're donating to the animal rescue so that I'll help you out," Zoe said. I couldn't argue with her there. Not even if I wanted to: It was like she'd grown and was staring down at me from a great distance, her voice like thunder. Or maybe it was that I was shrinking. "Do you know how many times I've tried to tell you how I felt? How I didn't want to do this? How I'm so upset and worried about Dogzilla? Have you been listening at *all*?"

I'd definitely shrunk. I felt like if I looked to the side, I'd see ants marching alongside me, their bitey heads shaking as they looked me straight in the eye. *You used to be tall, and you wasted it*, they'd tell me in what I somehow knew would be squeaky voices. *What have you done?*

"Aren't you going to say anything?" Zoe demanded. She was quivering with rage. If she were an ant, her antennae would be shivering over her head.

I wanted to say something—like how I hadn't meant to ignore her fear, it was just that mine was so all-consuming—but I didn't think she'd be able to hear me. I was too small.

She snorted. "Of course not. You're probably still

thinking about what you're going to do next for your plan. Poor, poor Ellie. Unable to ruin her own life, but still ruins everybody else's."

I waited for my insides to burst into flames, but it was like the opposite was happening. Everything felt kind of cold and damp and empty. Because Zoe hated me. My best friend. Hated *me*. She was yelling. At *me*.

There was nothing left of me. If she took a step toward me, she might squish me like a bug.

She hopped back onto the path. I shrank away. But she didn't come toward me. She flounced toward the house, her arms crossed, her black braids swinging behind her. Without even looking over her shoulder at me, she disappeared through the door, slamming it behind her, leaving me outside with the other ants.

I waited a minute, my heels sinking in the dirt. She didn't come back.

What was I supposed to do if she *never* came back? A vision of a Zoe-less future flashed before me. Me, sitting alone. Me, eating alone. Me, not talking to anyone, ever, until my voice withered from disuse.

And then, anger. Because Zoe was supposed to be my best friend. Why didn't she understand what a big deal this was for me? Of course I cared about Dogzilla. But there was no way her stress came close to mine.

Not ever. Normal people didn't understand what I was going through. Maybe people like her or Hannah had trouble sleeping the night before a big event, or got a little shaky or stammery when they had to talk in front of a crowd. But me? I'd get up on the bimah and choke to death. I'd black out in front of everyone and sweat so much liquid out of my body they'd never get the saltwater stain out of the red carpet. (There was still a stain from when Alina Rubin threw up while her class was leading Friday night services a few years ago.) Whatever I had going on in my body was literal death.

So even as I worried that I'd be alone forever, my resolve hardened. I wasn't going to apologize. I turned around and stalked back down the front path, my hands balled at my sides. Not just because Dogzilla's endless barking was giving me a headache. Because Zoe was the one who wasn't being a good friend. She should know how important this was for *me*.

CHAPTER 18

Mom was already off the phone when I got into the car, her lips pressed into a thin, pale line. She didn't ask me about Zoe, and I didn't ask her about Mrs. Goldblum's call. She didn't accuse me of destroying Carl's bar mitzvah with a food fight, and I didn't accuse her of ruining my life by hiring Mrs. Goldblum in the first place. So there were a lot of things not said in that car.

Not until we got home. Mom booked it into the kitchen, where Dad was already sitting with a bowl of cereal. Even though it was nighttime. Dad was a wild man. I drifted along behind her, trying not to make it obvious that I was in hot pursuit. She went immediately to the cabinet beside the stove for a tea bag. I grabbed a glass for water, letting it fill from the dispenser as slowly as I could. *Drip. Drip. Drip.*

Mom was telling Dad about her phone call in a rapid-fire burst of words. As I listened, relief dripped through me the same way the water was very slowly filling my cup. "She sounded angry, but all she said was that there was a sudden conflict on that date and that she was sorry, but she would have to bow out."

"Is she giving us our deposit back?" Dad asked, crunching loudly on cereal.

Mom's eyes widened. "Is that your biggest concern?"

Dad shrugged. "It was a pretty big chunk of change."

Mom shook her head. "I'd say the biggest concern is how we're going to feed all of our guests," she said. "There aren't any other kosher caterers in town."

My glass overflowed. I jumped with surprise as water splashed onto the floor.

Dad leaped to his feet. "Ellie!"

"Sorry," I squeaked, abandoning the full glass and scooting for the door before they could start asking me questions. It worked. I lurked on the other side of the doorway as they went back to each other.

"I don't know," Dad said. "Pizza?"

"It's not like we can get the pizza oven into the firehouse. That could start a fire."

"Hey, if it starts a fire, it's kind of the perfect place for it, right?" Dad joked.

I ran up to my room before Mom could get angry, giving myself a congratulatory fist pump. Operation Blatant Bacon had been a huge success for everyone and everything except Hannah's old dress, which was now definitely going in the garbage. You could only get so much caked-on steak sauce out.

I tried not to think about how the rest of the night had been much less of a success. About how Zoe was probably in her room right now methodically deleting all the photos we'd ever taken together. About how Mrs. Goldblum had spent hours making food now splattered over the walls, and Ms. Winters and the rest of the staff were probably still scrubbing tomato sauce out of the carpet.

Hannah popped out of her room. I suppressed a groan. "Hey," she said, leaning against her door frame. "How was your friend's bar— Oh my God!" Her eyes widened as she took in the state of my dress. "What *happened* to you?" Quick as a flash, her eyes narrowed to slits. "Did somebody do this to you? Who do I have to destroy?"

What was she— Oh. I remembered how she and my family thought my venue got canceled because somebody from school or wherever was bullying me. Hannah must have thought that someone at Carl's bar mitzvah spilled a plate of food on me as a horrible prank.

I snorted back a laugh and hunched over with guilt at the same time. I probably looked deranged. Hannah was staring at me like I looked deranged, anyway. "Nobody *did* this to me. There was a food fight."

"Oh no," she said sympathetically. "Your poor friend."

"Carl's not really my friend," I said. "And he loved it." I went to go into my room, but Hannah stepped into the hallway lightning fast, blocking my way. I suppressed a groan again. Did she have to ruin *everything*?

"I heard what you guys were talking about downstairs," she said. "About the caterer?" Of course she had. What, was she going to volunteer to make a hundred and fifty kosher meals all on her own? Because she probably could. She was Hannah, and Hannah could do anything.

Despite my annoyance with Hannah, a surge of triumph shot through me anyway. "Yeah," I said, trying to sound sad and not smug. "It looks like they canceled at the last minute."

Hannah pressed her lips together into one thin line, a look that echoed our mom so clearly that I blinked in surprise. "So you're not going to have a caterer for your bat mitzvah?"

I shrugged. "Guess not. But it's okay."

I went to move past her again, but she only leaned in. "Don't worry, Ellie," she said, her voice low and deadly, an odd tone for someone telling me not to worry. "Even if I have to make a hundred and fifty peanut butter sandwiches myself, you *will have that bat mitzvah party*."

Battle flashed in her eyes. I shivered. This must have been what soldiers charging into war felt like before their swords and shields started clanging.

Then Hannah stepped back, and she was normal Hannah again, which was still at least halfway on the scary scale. "I'll make sure of it," she said. "Because if you're going through all the work it takes to sing your haftorah and Torah portions and everything up there in front of everybody, that means you're an adult. And you deserve a party celebrating that, because you're special. You know that, right?"

I know I wasn't thinking of the word *special* the same way that she was, but I nodded anyway just to make her stop. And because my head was suddenly heavy with all the new thoughts running around in it. "Sure."

Finally she got out of the way. I scurried into my room and slammed the door behind me, flopping onto my bed.

From what Hannah had said, it was clear that my efforts to sabotage my bat mitzvah party wouldn't be enough. Even if I burned down the firehouse (which would be ironic) and bought out every single food source in a fifty-mile radius, Hannah would figure out some way to "celebrate" me. She'd probably build a tent in the ashes and create a fancy five-course kosher meal out of what she could find in our neighbors' pantries. And if that was true, I had to forget the party and go straight to the source. The service.

I couldn't get her words out of my head. *If you're going through all the work it takes to sing your haftorah and Torah portions and everything up there in front of everybody, that means you're an adult. And you deserve a party celebrating that, because you're special.* The party didn't matter anymore. I had to go down to the root of the bat mitzvah and kill the plant there: the actual ceremony itself.

The thought honestly made me queasy. I definitely didn't want a big party. But that didn't mean I didn't want to become a bat mitzvah. The bat mitzvah ceremony, haftorah and all, was how you became an adult in the Jewish religion. If I didn't have a bat mitzvah, could I ever become an adult?

Maybe becoming an adult meant dealing with all this stuff. Figuring out a way to make the hard things easier so that I could do them.

"Or maybe you just have to figure out a way that you don't have to do them at all," I firmly whispered to myself. Wasn't that what adults did all the time? Mom and Dad didn't want to clean the bathrooms, ever, so they hired someone to come twice a month and deep clean everything. And they were definitely, without a doubt, one hundred percent adults.

Still, I bet hiring someone to clean the bathrooms didn't make them feel bad. The way I felt bad right now. About stressing them out and making them sad. About Zoe being mad at me. About everybody thinking I was apparently the target of some horrific bullying campaign, when really the bully was me.

If Hannah was going to make sure I had a big party no matter what, as long as I completed my bat mitzvah, then I had to make sure I couldn't complete my bat mitzvah. No matter how queasy the thought made me. And I couldn't just wait for the day of and get up there and not say anything, because then the party and everything would be set up and ready to go. Hannah would probably paint the balloons blue—for sadness—and turn the whole thing into an actual pity party.

No, I had to do this ahead of time. Which meant sabotaging the service.

I moved the garbage can next to my bed, in case I threw up, and lay down. I had a lot of mental rehearsal to do.

CHAPTER 19

Most of the year, I had Hebrew school on Tuesdays and Thursdays from four to six p.m. Since school was out for the summer, Hebrew school was also out for the summer. However, those of us with bar and bat mitzvah lessons still had to go in for our lessons once a week with the cantor. Learning your haftorah and Torah portions waited for nothing, not even summer vacation.

While we had classrooms for Hebrew school, bat mitzvah lessons were held in the beit midrash—which literally means "a house of learning" but is actually a small room full of books tacked on to the side of the sanctuary. My dad dropped me off, and I went immediately to the playground.

I'd spent my entire childhood on this playground, or

at least it felt like that. Zooming down the slide after junior congregation in the beit midrash ended, as long as I was too young for the main services in the sanctuary. Going up and down on the seesaw with Hannah before or after Hebrew school. Propelling myself round and round on the little spinny thing when one of my parents had to stop in for a moment at temple.

For now, I sat on one of the swings and let my feet drag in the sand. I was getting a little big for the playground, I realized. But if I didn't have a bat mitzvah, I'd be a kid forever. I'd be trapped out here on the playground, getting stuck on the slide, forever being the bottom weight on the seesaw, while everybody else in my class got up and led services in the sanctuary.

Was that *really* what I wanted?

No. That wasn't the right question. Was it what I *needed*? It was. It definitely was. Even though . . . I'd done a whole lot lately that I didn't think I could. Like talk to strangers. Start a food fight. Confront the DJ. If I could do all those things with the help of deep breathing and rehearsing what I was going to say ahead of time, maybe I *could* handle making a speech in front of all my guests. Kissing the cheeks of hundreds of people I barely knew.

Singing my haftorah in front of practically every kid I'd ever met.

But I really, really didn't want to.

"Ellie?"

I looked up at the sound of my name. The cantor was looking at me from the door of the beit midrash, his light blue eyes twinkling in his wrinkled face.

Everybody knows what a rabbi is (in case you don't, the rabbi is basically the spiritual head of the synagogue), but I don't think anyone who isn't Jewish knows what a cantor is. To be honest, I still don't know exactly what a cantor's job description is. But our cantor is always up with the rabbi during services, doing most of the singing of prayers and the Torah portions if nobody else is there to do them. He also does all the bar and bat mitzvah lessons.

I followed him inside the beit midrash and closed the door behind me, leaving us in the dimness of the room. Usually I liked rooms with big windows and a lot of light, but something about the dimness of the beit midrash always calmed me. The light of the sun was filtered through stained-glass windows on the far side of the room, and everything smelled like the old books that lined the walls.

The cantor sat down at the long table, pulling out a chair for me. "How are you doing, Ellie?"

Usually I answered questions like that with an automatic "Good" or "Fine," but today I actually stopped and considered. How *was* I doing? Not great, both physically—my stomach was really queasy again—or mentally—the guilt I'd started feeling way back at the beginning of this whole plan had become a permanent weight in my stomach, and I was already feeling bad for what I was about to do.

I couldn't exactly tell him how I was feeling, but I didn't want to lie to the cantor. So I just gave him a shrug. He nodded like that meant something. "Let's get started, shall we?"

I sat down, then pulled out the green paper booklet containing my haftorah and placed it on the table before me. There's a new haftorah every week; each one is a selection from the books of Prophets, and most tell a story—mine features a song that long-ago King David sang to God, talking about how God saved him from his enemies. (It's actually pretty intense—think "devouring fire" and "huge thunderheads" saving David from the "coils of death." If you ask me, it would make a pretty great metal song.)

But I didn't open my book. "I was actually thinking we could talk about my speech," I said, folding my hands over the book so that I couldn't open it even if I wanted to. I took a deep breath. "That's kind of the most important part, isn't it? Everybody's going to be zoning out for the haftorah, but they're all going to be listening to my speech to hear what I've learned through this whole process. Why I'm ready to become an adult."

The cantor's forehead wrinkled. "I certainly won't be 'zoning out' during your haftorah. But go ahead. Tell me your thoughts."

I took in a deep breath, then let it all out in a long, low whoosh. "Okay. Here's what I'm thinking." I paused for maximum effect, just like I'd rehearsed. "I don't think it was God who saved King David from his enemies. I think it was aliens."

"Aliens?" The cantor's voice was carefully measured. I'd anticipated a confused response like this, so I was good to go on.

"Yes. Aliens. It was the aliens who sent their 'devouring fire' and 'huge thunderheads' to save David before zooming to the ground in their shiny silver UFOs. Obviously King David was grateful they saved his life and all, so they made a bargain with him that he wouldn't tell anyone else about them so that they could continue their work on Earth."

"Their . . . work on Earth?"

I flipped my hair in the way I'd seen the popular girls do at school. It just made my hair fall in my face, which meant I had to flip it again just to see. "Yep. You didn't believe the Torah when it said our ancestors built the pyramids, right?" I laughed like that was ridiculous. "No, obviously it was the aliens. They bred with our ancestors, actually, so all of us Jews are really part alien." That echoed some serious conspiracy theories I'd heard in the past about Jews actually being aliens or lizard people, but I pushed those thoughts away. "Wait until you hear about the alien influence on American society."

The cantor's expression grew more and more troubled as I talked on. By the time I finished up, my head was pulsing in time with my heart. Maybe that was the sign of death.

Eliana Rachel Katz, age twelve, died at her—

No. My thoughts from Zoe's house intruded. I'd thought I was going to die a lot. I'd imagined all these obituaries for myself. But I'd never actually died. What was the absolute worst thing that could happen right now? Not death. The cantor would be unhappy with me, and he'd think I was an idiot. I could handle that. Plenty of people around the world were already unhappy with me and didn't like me just because I was Jewish.

I waited for the cantor to tell me what a terrible job I'd done. To yell at me for being a garbage person. To tell me I was clearly not mature enough to have a bat mitzvah and may God have mercy on my soul.

But he only raised his eyebrows. "Is there anything you want to talk about, Ellie?"

"Just the aliens," I said innocently. "Is something wrong?"

He stared at me. "That's what I'd like to ask you," he said. "Is something wrong, Ellie?"

That's how you know it's serious: When an adult says your name over and over again, like they want to make absolutely sure you know who they're talking to.

"Nothing's wrong," I said, trying to sound breezy, except I'm pretty sure I sounded like I was choking. "Why, is there a problem with my speech? I think it was pretty good. And I think it'll sound even better when I get up there on the bimah and make it in front of *everyone*." I raised my own eyebrows at him, a challenge.

The silence that followed was so loud I could hear it. The air-conditioning vent rattled above me. Something buzzed in the walls. I swallowed over and over again until my throat was dry as dust, avoiding his eyes the whole time.

And then the cantor sighed. "What are you doing, Ellie?"

I shrugged weakly. "I don't know what you mean."

"Talk to me." I didn't talk. "Or I can refer you to—"

"I don't need to talk to anyone!" I didn't care if it was bad manners to interrupt. He wasn't getting it. "If you think I'm doing such a bad job, then I guess I won't be able to have my bat mitzvah after all."

"Is that really what you want?" His voice was gentle, and I hated it. *Hated* it. I wanted him to yell at me. To scream at me. That was what I deserved right now.

Yes. It was what I wanted. I couldn't have a bat mitzvah party, which meant I couldn't complete a bat mitzvah service. It was as simple as that.

"You know as well as I do that becoming an adult in the Jewish religion is marked by having a bar or bat mitzvah," the cantor continued. "Are you afraid of becoming a Jewish adult?"

I wasn't so much afraid of that. I knew it didn't really mean not being a kid—I'd be stuck as a kid until I moved out of my parents' home. And I loved being Jewish. The sense of history. The feeling that we'd survived so much throughout it. And yeah, even the feeling of exclusivity, because while you could convert to Judaism and we welcomed converts as if they were born Jews, it was a long, difficult process, so there weren't a lot of people who did it. It was like I was part of a club I'd been born into, and that all my ancestors had been in, too. When I said the words of the Kaddish or the Shema, I could almost hear all my ancestors saying it along with me.

I raised my chin stubbornly. "I don't know what you mean. There's nothing wrong with my speech."

The cantor sighed. I looked at him. He looked at me. His eyes felt like they could see right through the openings of my own eyes into my brain. I shifted mine away and stared at his forehead, a trick one of my teachers had taught us for when we didn't want to look someone in the eye but still wanted it to look like we were.

"Maybe we need a break," he said.

I wasn't afraid of being a Jewish adult. All it really meant was that I'd be officially counted in some of our rituals, where a child didn't count, and that I'd be expected to fulfill the commandments of our religion, which I basically already did. What else did it mean to be a Jewish adult?

Maybe being an adult means facing your problems instead of trying as hard as you can to avoid them, whispered that annoying little voice.

I shook my head, dismissing the thought. I knew I couldn't handle the bat mitzvah party my family was planning, so I was making sure I wouldn't have one. I *was* facing my problems. Wasn't I?

Or is facing your problems actually having a hard conversation with your parents? Maybe sometimes the first step in facing your problems is admitting that you have problems so that you can ask for help?

"You don't want to take a break?" the cantor asked. Right. I'd shaken my head, so he'd assumed I was saying no. "Because I have to be frank with you, Ellie. You can't get up and give that speech, and I think you know that."

He sighed. "It's okay if you're nervous," he said. "I've been doing this for more years than you've been alive, and it's a big deal. It's hard to get up there and talk to the entire congregation." Was he trying to make me feel better? Because it wasn't working. "Maybe we can figure out a good compromise."

But we couldn't. Not without having that hard conversation with my family. So I just stared at that spot on his forehead, unmoving, until he sighed again. "Our time is up," he said. "Go home, get some sleep. I'll give you a call tomorrow, okay?"

I remained deep in thought as I walked outside. Because maybe facing my problems wasn't what I was doing.

It definitely wasn't what I was doing with Zoe. I'd apologize, I decided. I was going to see her tomorrow morning at the library, and there, I'd tell her exactly how sorry I was.

I could face that problem, especially if it meant leaving the big one alone.

CHAPTER 20

When my mom dropped me off at the library the next morning, all my veins were running hot with determination (and also blood, in the literal sense). I was a few minutes late, which meant Zoe was almost definitely waiting inside. I ran over my plan in my head as the automatic glass doors parted dramatically before me. I'd convince her to go to a quiet spot in the stacks, no matter if she refused to even say hello to me. Then I'd look her in the eye and tell her how sorry I was and that I missed her and needed her, and we'd be best friends again. There. Easy.

Andrea ran up to me as I entered the children's section. There seemed to be even more books strewn everywhere than usual, the noise at a louder volume than I remembered. "Ellie! There you are!" Her hair, usually in a high, tight ponytail, was loose today, frazzled into a cloud around her face. "The kids are wild today!"

My eyes darted from side to side, looking for Zoe. She wasn't hiding behind the giant stuffed bear lording over the easy readers. She wasn't crouching in the picture book stacks seeking out a book or two for storytime.

"Your friend's not here today!" Andrea said.

My heart just about stopped. I saw my plan crumbling around me into dust. "What?"

"YOUR FRIEND'S NOT HERE TODAY!" Andrea shouted, like the problem was just that I hadn't heard her. Her voice quieted as she continued. "She called out this morning! Something about a family emergency!"

My heart definitely stopped, which meant I would probably die—

No. Something was still horribly wrong with my internal organs, but it wouldn't kill me. I wasn't going to die right now.

Not the way Dogzilla most likely had. Because what else could this "family emergency" be? Dogzilla was her family, and he had cancer, and now he had to be dead, and I hadn't been there for it. I hadn't been there for Zoe. The guilt covered me like a heavy woolen blanket in the middle of summer.

Maybe that's why, when Andrea said, "Which means you've got storytime all on your own!" I barely even felt the stirrings of panic beneath guilt's heavy weight. This felt like penance. Atonement. Punishment.

I nodded and somehow dragged my heavy limbs along to the children's section. I picked out two random picture books, mostly because they looked slightly shorter than the ones around them. I assembled the beanbags and cushions for the little kids, and I took my seat in the front, and only when all the kids started rushing over did my heart start to flutter with nerves.

Deep breaths, Ellie. Deep breaths. I focused on breathing in and out, slowly and surely, then flicked my eyes down to the covers of the picture books in my hands. The top one was something about a stolen hat. *You do not have to make up a story about a stolen hat,* I told myself. *It's like an email. It's already right there on the page. All you have to do is read what's already there.*

The breaths started to come a little easier. *And what's the absolute worst thing that could happen? You're not going to die (barring freak meteorite strike into the roof of the library that makes the roof collapse right on you). All that will happen is that these little kids will laugh at you and/or yell at you. And so what if they do? They're just little kids. No one cares what they think.*

So I took one more deep breath, opened the cover of the book, and started reading out loud. My heart fluttered nauseously the whole time, and sweat made my palms and armpits and neck sticky and gross, but the words kept coming out of my mouth. They were probably too quick, and they probably weren't loud enough, but they came out.

I was shaking by the time I closed the second book, but I was still alive. "Everybody thank Ellie for doing a wonderful job!" Andrea said from behind me. I jumped in my chair, because I had no idea when she'd showed up. For someone who spoke only in exclamation points, she could be very sneaky.

The kids cheered, then jumped up and zoomed away, hopefully to their parents and not to mess up the kids' section more. I went to go return the storytime books to the shelf, but Andrea stepped in front of me, her smile so wide she actually looked a little deranged. "Ellie, you did such a great job!" she said.

I almost rolled my eyes. My job had not been great.

Maybe Andrea saw me thinking that, because she said, more quietly, "I'm very proud of you."

And maybe it was that she hadn't said it with an exclamation point, or maybe it was that she sounded so sincere, but it made me give her a real, genuine smile.

That smile only lasted through half an hour of reshelving books, though, before I started worrying about Zoe again. Should I text her? I hadn't messaged her since our fight. Or would it be weird to text her without resolving our issues or whatever?

Maybe I should ask my dad to drop me off at Zoe's house on our way home from the library. Yes, I would do that. He wouldn't mind a pit stop. He and Zoe's dad were friends. They nerded out about Dungeons & Dragons together, which Zoe and I always made fun of even though we secretly wanted to play.

So I ran toward my dad's car as soon as I saw it. "Dad," I said breathlessly as I climbed into the back seat. "Can we . . ."

I trailed off as he turned around. He was looking at me sternly, a look he almost never had on his face. And . . . there was my mom in the passenger seat. Also looking at me sternly.

"Ellie," Dad said. "I found something very interesting under your mattress while I was making your bed."

Oh no. The invitations. I'd totally forgotten about them.

"And," continued Mom, "we got a call from the cantor this afternoon."

Oh. Oh no.

"It made us decide to investigate the venue cancellation, which led to a call to Ms. Winters," said Dad.

Oh. No. A pit of dread opened up in my stomach, threatening to swallow me whole.

Mom asked, "Care to explain yourself?"

I didn't. I kept my mouth shut the whole way home.

CHAPTER 21

My parents didn't push it on the ride home. I almost let their silence lull me into feeling safe, even as they got home and ushered me into the kitchen. Maybe they wouldn't push it further. Maybe they'd realize how obviously stressed out I was and let it be.

That lasted about as long as it took for us to assemble around the kitchen table. Mom cupped her mug of tea. Dad poured me a glass of water. He poured himself a mixture of blue Gatorade and orange soda. I drank my glass of water. He took a sip of his drink and grimaced.

Then the questions started. "Ellie," my mom began. "Why would you hide your bat mitzvah invitations? Why would you tell the cantor you wanted to do your bat mitzvah speech about aliens?"

"And why would you pretend to be your mother and tell the venue you'd died?" Dad said. He shuddered at the thought, which made me feel kind of sad. "We're not angry yet. Just confused. Tell us your thoughts."

I kept my lips pressed firmly together into a thin line as they stared at me. The back of my neck started to heat up. I wished I had another glass of water.

"Ellie," Mom said a little bit more sternly. "You can't just sit there. You need to answer us."

But I couldn't. It was like I'd forgotten every word I'd ever learned.

Dad pounded a fist on the table. His radioactive-looking beverage jumped. "Ellie! This is important! Don't you know how much money we've spent? How much time we've spent planning? Why would you . . ." He trailed off, like he'd forgotten all his words, too.

So Mom took over. "Are you being bullied?" she asked. "Or did something else happen that forced you to do this?"

They went on asking questions, and I went on not giving them any answers. The whole time, my heart beat steadily. The fire burned at its usual low level. I felt . . . okay. I mean, yeah, really nervous. But mostly okay.

It actually felt kind of good to have it all out in the open, somehow.

My parents both put their elbows on the table at once and focused both sets of eyes on me, like they were lasers trying to crack a safe. "Please, Ellie," Dad said, and Mom finished with "Just tell us why."

I couldn't. There was nothing I could say that they'd understand. Nothing at all. They'd be like Zoe or Hannah. *I get it, Ellie. Everyone gets a little nervous sometimes. Let's talk about it.* They didn't get it. There was nothing to talk about when your insides were literally on fire and you couldn't breathe. Like, I hadn't died doing any of this other stuff, but none of that approached the bat mitzvah stuff they wanted me to do.

So I jumped up and ran to my room, slamming the door behind me.

CHAPTER 22

All alone, I could focus a little easier. They knew now. There was no taking that back. Maybe I could rehearse a conversation that would tell them what they needed to know without thinking I was an actual nutcase.

So when my door cracked open, I wasn't thrilled. I was already annoyed that my parents wouldn't install locks on our doors. "Leave me alone."

The door kept opening. My parents were usually pretty respectful of my space in my room, which meant it could be none other than—

Hannah stepped inside, her hair up in one of those messy buns that took her about two seconds to pull together yet somehow always looked like the ones celebrities wore to go grocery shopping. She had on one of her old Kadima T-shirts, which reminded me that she was supposed to be out talking to old people again today.

"I just got home and was walking in the front door when I heard Mom and Dad yelling at you," she said without any greetings. "Is it true? That *you've* been the one sabotaging your *own* bat mitzvah?"

I scowled, staring past her into the hallway. If I didn't say anything, maybe she'd just go away.

It didn't work. She stepped inside, closed the door behind her, and stood in front of it with her arms crossed, like she was a security guard and thought I was going to make a run for it. Stupid Hannah. If I were going to make a run for it, I'd definitely go out the window.

"Are you being normal Ellie quiet or is this guilty quiet?" Hannah continued. "Because it kind of seems like the second one."

Could I go out the window without breaking my leg?

"Come on, Ellie. Just say something."

I didn't care. I'd break both my legs to get away from this conversation.

"*Ellie.*"

My fists clenched at my sides. My jaw clenched on my face. The only thing that didn't clench was my voice, which launched itself at Hannah with the force of a rock shattering a window. "SHUT UP!"

Hannah's mouth fell open. "What?"

"SHUT. UP." Now that the words were coming out, I couldn't stop them. It felt almost like throwing up. "STOP TRYING TO FIX ME. YOU CAN'T FIX ME. I'LL NEVER BE LIKE YOU."

Just like throwing up, spilling all those words out of me was actually making me feel a little bit better. So I kept going. "YOU'VE ALREADY RUINED ENOUGH OF MY LIFE. STOP TRYING TO RUIN THE REST OF IT."

I turned and crossed my arms, hunching my shoulders over them. I felt like one of those roly-poly bugs with the soft insides and the hard shells on their back that curled in on themselves when they were feeling threatened. Oddly enough, I didn't feel like I was on fire. There were figurative flames of anger shooting out of me, but I didn't actually feel like I'd burn up.

"Ellie . . ." Hannah's voice was tiny.

I didn't want to look at her or hear what she had to say. So I kept on yelling, this time focusing on that stupid photo board she'd made me. "JUST GET AWAY FROM

ME. GET AWAY FROM ME AND LEAVE ME ALONE."

If someone had yelled that at me, I'd be frantically thinking of escape. So I expected to hear Hannah stumbling over her feet in her rush to get out.

But I didn't hear anything. Maybe she'd crept away so quietly it didn't register as sound waves? I turned around slowly, hoping against hope that she was gone and I wouldn't have to deal with any of these emotions she was bringing out.

She was still there. And not even glaring at me. Her face was buried in her hands, and her shoulders were shaking. Now that I was facing her, I could hear her: It sounded like she was panting for breath, almost, like she couldn't get enough air.

And it was that noise that made me take a step toward her. Because I knew that feeling of not being able to get enough air.

Maybe it was a genetic trait. Maybe we both had it. "Hannah?" I said tentatively, moving closer to her. "Are you . . . crying?"

She took her face out of her hands immediately, wiping her eyes with the backs of them. Her eyes were red and a little shiny, but there weren't any tears falling. "No," she told me. "It's something I do when I feel overwhelmed. When I feel like I might get buried under everything I have to do, I block out the world and breathe."

That . . . that sounded a lot like what *I* did. When I closed my eyes and took deep breaths to calm myself down.

I sat down on my bed. "Fine. We can talk." But it didn't make any sense. Perfect, social Hannah, using the same coping mechanism as me? No. No way.

She took a seat on the other end of the bed. Even though it wasn't like my bed was that big. If I reached my arm out over the cheery pink comforter, I'd hit her.

"I just don't *get* it," Hannah said. Her hands were clasped in her lap. "Why are you saying these things?" Her lower lip trembled, like she actually might cry. "I *love* you, you idiot. I was trying to make sure you had the absolute *perfect* bat mitzvah party, just like I did. Why wouldn't you want it?"

My instinct was to hide. To let out a squeak like a scared mouse and scurry under my bed to live among the mothballs and dust bunnies for a while. As a mouse, I would be their queen.

But what was the worst-case scenario here? I wasn't

going to die (not unless there was a major freak accident like a tree falling on the roof exactly where I happened to be sitting, but that would happen whether I talked to Hannah or not). Hannah was already upset with me—could she even get more upset? I guessed that was the worst-case scenario. That she'd be madder at me than she already was. And I could live with that.

Okay. That was already making things feel easier. I closed my eyes and took a deep breath, visualizing what I wanted to say. She sat patiently waiting, like she knew exactly what I was doing. I wanted to make sure I got everything right.

But the way I was going to do that made her sound like a villain, and I didn't want to upset her more. Seeing how upset she was right now, it seemed like she really had meant well, even if she'd been oblivious. So I needed to rephrase this to not to hurt her feelings.

I didn't know if that would be possible. But I had to try.

I took another deep, calming breath in the dark, then opened my eyes. Without realizing it, I'd mirrored her position, folding my hands in my lap. "I appreciate the effort and I know you mean well," I said, my new addition. "But I'm not you. I'm not outgoing and social and perfect like you." I might have tried not to hurt her, but she still looked like I'd reached over and slapped her across the face.

Still, I had to keep going. My words tumbled out in a rush. "I don't want a big blowout like you had. I don't want to have to sing and make speeches and dance in front of a bunch of strangers and run around playing games with kids I barely know."

I continued, "I know you tried to give me the perfect bat mitzvah, and that was nice of you. But I'm a different person, and I want something different. Something small and low-key. So . . . I tried to make that happen. Except you kept coming in and trying to fix things."

I let the silence fall over us, thick and smothering. But I let it sit, because I could tell Hannah was thinking. Her eyebrows were scrunched. Her lips were pursed. I held my breath.

Finally she sighed. "You're right." Her hands opened up, her arms falling to her sides. "You're totally right. I was selfish, and stupid. I was thinking about what *I* wanted, not what you wanted. And we're different people. So it makes sense that we would want different things."

It was like I suddenly sprouted a third lung. Because I

hadn't always been able to breathe this deeply or easily, had I? "So you understand?" I said hopefully.

"Mostly," she answered. "Though I don't really get why you didn't just *tell* us this in the first place. Wouldn't that be easier than faking your own death?"

"I didn't exactly fake my own death," I said. "And . . ." I trailed off, because I had no idea how to answer her. In theory, yeah, her idea sounded a lot easier. A lot more logical. But it didn't capture what I had going on inside me, which wasn't logical. I sighed. "There's something wrong with me," I said, and I just spilled it all. From what happened at her bat mitzvah to now, and why I couldn't disappoint them, because I'd die.

For someone who'd just learned she nearly killed her own little sister with a fiery cake, Hannah did not look particularly concerned. "Oh, it sounds like a panic attack," she said.

I shook my head. "Zoe said that, too, but it wasn't just panic. It was like a heart attack. It was—"

Hannah interrupted me. "It really sounds like a panic attack. One of the girls in my grade gets them sometimes. It sounds scary." A tiny smile. "You know, you should talk to Mom and Dad about it to figure out what's going on.

They'll understand. It sounds like you need some help, and that's nothing to be embarrassed about." She raised her eyebrows. "Seriously. Everybody needs help sometimes. Like, you said I was perfect. That's absurd. Nobody's perfect."

I rolled my eyes.

Hannah snorted. "I saw that. So I'm an extrovert. I like being around people. It doesn't mean that I don't get anxious sometimes! Everybody does. And you know, you might think I'm super social, but it's not always easy." She scooted close to me and leaned in, like she was worried about someone overhearing. "You remember my friend Mia? From middle school?"

"Yeah." Mia had slept over our house all the time. I'd fallen asleep more nights than I could count to the sound of her and Hannah giggling across the hall.

But come to think of it, I hadn't seen Mia in a while.

Hannah's lips twisted. "It turned out that she wasn't really a good friend. I found out she'd been making fun of me behind my back. Of how loud my laugh is and how I'm 'too ugly to be so confident.'"

"You're not," I said. "No way."

Hannah shrugged. "It doesn't actually matter. I think

she'd say the same things no matter what I looked like," she said. "But it really hit me. When I saw those screenshots, they literally felt like Mia had kicked me in the stomach. With a high-heeled shoe on. So I stopped laughing so loud." She got quiet. I waited for her to go on, to tell me about how she'd conquered her insecurities and triumphed over Mia, but she stayed quiet.

So I realized that was it. That she hadn't conquered or triumphed over anything. She was still dealing with it. Hiding it.

"So planning your bat mitzvah was kind of a distraction for me," she said. "I couldn't make my own life great, but I could make yours great. I realized my best friend kind of sucked, but I could help *you* make friends." She sighed. "Except I'd been thinking about what was best for me, not for you. And I'm sorry. I'll help you talk to Mom and Dad."

I wasn't really a hugger. But I leaned over and hugged her anyway.

When I finally pulled away, she asked, "Should we go down now?"

The yes was on the tip of my tongue, but something held it back. Because some of what she'd said really hit home. About hiding her own problems. About focusing on what she wanted over what somebody else wanted.

"In a little while," I said. "Can you give me a few minutes?"

She nodded and stood. "Of course. I'll be waiting." She headed out into the hallway, closing my door behind her. I took a deep breath and grabbed my phone.

Zoe didn't answer my first call, but she couldn't put me off that easily. It took seven tries of waiting for all her rings to run out, but I finally got her huffy "What?" in my ear.

There was no sweeter sound. "Zoe, I'm sorry," I said, then blinked in surprise. I'd thought it would be a lot harder to get those words out.

She met me with a cautious silence. "Sorry for what?"

"For being a bad friend," I said. I sniffed.

Zoe sighed in my ear. "Oh, Ellie. You're not a bad friend."

"I kind of was, though," I told her. "I ignored everything you were saying so I could keep going with what I wanted. I'm really sorry about Dogzilla, and I want to be there for the funeral. I'm so sorry he's dead."

Zoe was quiet for a minute. I worried that maybe she'd

hung up and I hadn't heard the beep, until she said, "What? Funeral? Dogzilla's not dead!"

"But I thought . . . the family emergency . . ."

"My great-aunt was in a car accident," Zoe said. "She's fine. Just a few broken bones. But we had to go visit her in the hospital."

Relief knocked me over like a wave. "Oh, Zoe, that's great!" I exclaimed. Then realized what I'd just said. "I mean, not that your great-aunt was in a car accident. That sucks. But it's great that Dogzilla isn't dead!" It meant things weren't too late. That I could still be there for her. I lowered my tone into something less morbidly gleeful. "I'm still really sorry about Dogzilla. Who is alive. I don't know what it feels like, but I know it's hard for you. I want to be there for you the way you've been there for me."

She was quiet for another minute . . . until the words starting bursting out. "He's an old dog. They say we're not going to do anything until he's in pain." From the tone of her voice, I knew that by "do anything," she meant putting him to sleep. "But it's so hard. He's such a good dog, and he doesn't know anything is wrong. So I'm trying to pet him as much as I can, and play with him, and . . ."

She went on and on, and I listened to every word.

CHAPTER 23

But I couldn't talk to Zoe forever. My parents were still waiting downstairs, and I knew Hannah was in the hallway, waiting for me to come out so that she could stick her nose in—no, so that she could try to help. Because that was what she'd been doing.

Even if she wasn't very good at it.

My parents were waiting right where I had left them, sitting at the kitchen table with their drinks, though my mom's tea had grown cold and my dad's weird orange-soda-and-blue-Gatorade mixture was looking unappetizingly brownish gray. They looked up at me as Hannah and I walked in. This was when I'd usually start to sweat, maybe feel a little shaky, but somehow I was drawing on a deep reserve of calm within me. Or maybe it was the sense of calm radiating from my sister as she stood beside me.

I took a deep breath. I knew what I had to say, and yet the words wouldn't come. I had no idea where to start.

"Mom and Dad," Hannah prompted. "Ellie has something she needs to say to you. About some stuff she's been going through."

And just like that, I knew exactly what to focus on. *Maybe she's better at helping than I thought.* I took another deep breath and opened my mouth.

"It's like sometimes there's a fire in me and I get really sweaty and I can't breathe and I think I'm going to die," I said. My voice was tiny, but I knew the words themselves were strong. "I knew I couldn't have a bat mitzvah like you were planning. I just couldn't. It felt like I was going to die."

Mom sniffled. She reached up and swiped at the corner of her eye. Great. Now I felt awful for making my mom cry.

Still, I had to go on. "So I thought up a bunch of ways to make it so that . . . so that I wouldn't have to have that bat mitzvah. All by myself." I wasn't going to let Zoe go down with me. Not after what I did to her. "But each time

I tried, things just got worse. And worse. I felt really bad every time."

Mom was still sniffling. Dad glared at me and thundered, "Why didn't you just *tell* us?"

He made it sound so easy. "I couldn't," I said softly. "I didn't think you'd understand. Nobody else did. And . . . you'd already put so much work into planning it."

His eyebrows made a V over his nose. "We can't read your mind, Ellie! We want you to be happy, but you have to tell us what happy means to you!"

"Don't yell at her," Hannah said, which was good, because I was going to dissolve into tears like Mom if I kept getting yelled at. "What matters is that she's telling you now."

Dad took a deep breath. His face relaxed. "You're right. I'm sorry, Ellie. Keep going."

That made me feel a little better. I mean, not great, because Mom was still crying. But a little less awful. So I went on. I told them everything. Well, almost everything—I left out Zoe and her part in it. But I started at Hannah's bat mitzvah, when the cake almost killed me, and ended with me standing in front of them right now.

Mom wiped her eyes and sat up straight. "Ellie, do you know where I go every other Wednesday afternoon?"

I had no idea. "Work?"

She shook her head. "I go to therapy. And I think you should go, too."

Therapy? Me? Just like Hannah, they didn't get it. "You don't seem to understand," I told her. "I don't need to go sit on some psychologist's couch and talk to them about all my problems. It's physical. I told you, it's like I'm going to—"

"I have anxiety, and it sounds like you might, too," Mom interrupted, even though she always told us not to interrupt *her*. "I'll let the therapist make the formal diagnosis, but the sweating? The shaking? The panic attacks, and the being unable to speak to new people? Those all sound like anxiety, and we can get you help for that."

But . . .

"It's okay if you don't like getting up in front of big crowds. I don't, either," Mom said. "And I'm sorry we tried to make you do that. But it also sounds like the anxiety—if that's what it is—is interfering with your life. You should be able to talk to other people and make new friends. And even if you don't like it and try to avoid it, there are occasions where you'll *have* to talk in front of other people."

She was right. As much as I hated to admit it.

Maybe I *could* do my bat mitzvah. I'd learned I could do a lot more than I thought I could, after all. But that didn't change the fact that I didn't want to. Maybe . . . maybe I shouldn't keep quiet and out of the way entirely, like I'd been doing, but that didn't mean I suddenly had to jump into the spotlight. Maybe there was a nice place in the middle there I could carve out.

She smiled. "So we'll take you to therapy, and we'll get you some help."

I nodded, too emotional to say anything. There was a fist lodged in my throat.

"Sounds good," Dad said. "And once everybody's happy and healthy, then we'll talk about consequences for your behavior."

"Great." That was Hannah. She sat down at the table and clapped her hands together, then folded them in front of her. "So! It sounds like we have a backyard bat mitzvah to plan." She grinned at me. "Let's get started."

EPILOGUE

A couple of months later, the cantor smiled down at me. "Ellie, are you ready?"

I gave him a firm nod. "Ready."

Before I looked at my notes, though, I closed my eyes. I took a deep breath. I reminded myself that with the amount of times I'd rehearsed this, I could probably do this without any notes at all.

Then I opened my eyes and leaned into the microphone, staring out at all the eyes staring back at me. There weren't actually so many. Definitely fewer than two hundred and forty-seven, and I knew most of them well.

"My haftorah is about King David," I started. The crowd rustled. I stared at Hannah, pretending I was giving the speech entirely to her. The flames inside were definitely burning, but not enough to scorch my throat or stop me from speaking. She smiled encouragingly at me. I licked my lips and continued, "It talks about how he was facing all these hardships in battle."

Getting here hadn't exactly been easy. Not even literally—there was a lot of traffic on the way to temple this morning, and I had to wonder if my bat mitzvah would go forward without me. But here as in my mental state, too.

Sure, my parents were supportive. But that didn't mean I didn't have to make up for what I'd done. I had to write out an apology to Mrs. Goldblum, where I offered to volunteer my help at her next few events. And apologize to the DJ. I also wrote one to my parents, with a thank-you in there for donating some of the money to the animal rescue after all. And then there was therapy, which actually wasn't so bad. I'd figured out some ways of dealing with my anxiety—because it turned out that's what it is, not actual flames, as much as it felt that way—on my own, but therapy helped even more.

"For a while, David thought all was lost," I said. "And then he saw the hand of God reaching down through the fire and chaos of battle, and he was rescued."

After a few weeks of therapy was when Mom, Dad,

my new therapist, and I came up with a more fitting punishment. I was being opposite-grounded—instead of being forced to stay at home and be alone, I was being forced to go out and be around people. And I was doing some of the forcing myself, because I knew it was something I had to do. It started with me going to one Kadima event every other week.

It had been stressful at first, but it wasn't so bad anymore. Not now that I was getting to know everyone. I was even friendly with Sophie, who Hannah had tried to matchmake me with.

I smiled at Sophie in the second row. She smiled back, braces gleaming in the light. Next to her, Eva Karp and Jana Hart waved and gave me a thumbs-up. I gave them a tiny wave back, ignoring Danny Cohen, Carl Meier, and Todd Germaine arm-wrestling behind them.

"The thought of being plucked from danger is a nice one," I said. "But for those of us who aren't the king of ancient Israel, God's hand is in the hand of those who rescue themselves."

Later on, I stood in a receiving line in my backyard, greeting guests as they arrived. My parents and I had bargained ourselves down to a reasonable number: the kids in my Hebrew school class, plus the thirty or so relatives and family friends I actually knew. (Sorry, Uncle Barry. You and your eye patch had to stay home.) I fixed a smile on my face and replied to their *Mazel tov*s and *congratulations*es with one of the three responses I'd rehearsed with my family and my therapist. *Thank you so much!*, *You're very kind!*, and *I appreciate it!*

Mom's cousin reached out to squeeze my hands, surprising me. She was the last in line, and the savory smells of the pizza oven warming up were already starting to drift by the seated guests—I could see Zoe wiggling in her chair, ready to dash over as soon as they announced they were ready. "Mazel tov, dear," she said, and then added, "I can't wait to see your bat mitzvah announcement in the temple newsletter!"

I'd helped write it, so I knew how it would go:

```
Eliana Rachel Katz, age twelve, became
a bat mitzvah this past Saturday
morning. "We're so incredibly proud
of her," her parents gushed. "Me too!"
said her sister, Hannah. Her guests
thoroughly enjoyed the unique touches
```

of a pizza oven for dinner and an ice
cream truck for dessert.

The bat mitzvah announcement asked if I had any quotes to add, but I declined. Just because I could speak in front of people now didn't mean I wanted to, or that I always had to. I still preferred to be on the quiet side and stay out of the spotlight as much as possible. Therapy wasn't a magical fix, and some things might always be a little harder for me.

But that was okay. I could live with it. I *wanted* to live with it. And I could do the hard things now when it really counted.

"It's time for the cake ceremony!" Dad announced. Zoe slumped into her seat, groaning, her eyes fixed on the pizza oven. Hiding my smile, I made my way to the front of the group, where my dog-shaped cake waited. It wasn't just dog-shaped. Dogzilla's snout smiled up at me as I stuck a candle right into his eye.

My Dogzilla cake might have been a Zoe request. No, he wasn't dead. She just thought a Dogzilla cake would be awesome. She was right.

The crowd watched me as I recited the poems that

would call each of the selected family members, friends, or groups up to light their candle. My Hebrew school class, chattering excitedly among themselves about how a pizza-oven-and-ice-cream-truck bat mitzvah was the best thing they'd ever heard of. ("I'm totally doing this for mine," Sophie told me.) Various cousins, dancing up to the tune of "We Are Family" (the perennial bat mitzvah song). The cantor, beaming down at me so proudly. ("I'm glad to see the aliens didn't come down and transport you away for experimentation," he said, so maybe he hadn't totally forgotten my first speech.)

The fire before me continued to grow, blazing higher with every additional candle. Zoe, bouncing up to give me a tight hug and reaching fearlessly over the flames. Hannah, telling me how incredibly glad she was that I was her little sister. My parents, saying through tears that they were so, so proud of me and all I'd accomplished.

After that, I was left alone behind the cake of fire, peering at all my friends and relatives through the roaring blaze. My nemesis, back from Hannah's bat mitzvah to haunt me afresh.

I gave the cake of fire a hard look. "Nice try," I told it.

I smiled, leaned forward, and blew those candles out.

ACKNOWLEDGMENTS

I've dealt with anxiety my whole life, though for the most part it hasn't been as bad as Ellie's. I'm extremely fortunate to be surrounded by a team that made writing and publishing this book much less anxiety-inducing than it could have been—you might even say they're a foolproof, one-hundred-percent-perfect, no-way-they-can-fail-me group.

First of all, thank you to my incredible editors, Abigail McAden and Talia Seidenfeld. Ellie wouldn't be herself without the two of you. A special *toda rabah* to Talia for approaching me with the idea of a girl with anxiety who sabotages her own bat mitzvah, which sang to my heart and to the kid I used to be. Thank you to Dr. Rachel Busman from Child Mind Institute Medical Practice for your sensitivity read. And thank you so much to the rest of the team at Scholastic who brought this book into the world—Jessica White, Yaffa Jaskoll, Jordana Kulak, Julia Eisler, Rachel Feld, Josh Berlowitz, Jackie Hornberger,

Beka Wallin, Jody Corbett, and everybody else who had a hand in it.

A million thanks to my inimitable agent, Merrilee Heifetz. There's no one else I'd rather have on my side in this business. Thank you also to her wonderful assistant, Rebecca Eskildsen, and the rest of the team at Writers House.

Finally, a big thank-you to all the friends and family who support me, especially Jeremy Bohrer. I don't know what I'd do without you.

ABOUT THE AUTHOR

Amanda Panitch spent most of her childhood telling stories to her four younger siblings, trying both to make them laugh and to scare them too much to sleep. Now she lives in New York City, where she writes dark, funny stories for teens, kids, and the pigeons that nest on her apartment balcony. Visit Amanda online at amandapanitch.com.